CLAIM

OFF-LIMITS #3

PIPER LAWSON

PIPER LAWSON BOOKS

Published by Piper Lawson Books

Content editing by Becca Mysoor
Line and copy editing by Erica Russikoff
Cover photography by Regina Wamba

Claim (verb):

To demand or take as the rightful owner.

1

OLIVIA

The room tilts under my feet.

Expelled.

A moment ago, I was elated at the news that Sawyer had been granted a reprieve and would be allowed to stay at Russell.

But it turns out he's the only one the committee is inviting to stay.

"I can't be expelled," I blurt. "I did nothing wrong."

The dean shifts back on his heels, as if my response is tiresome if expected. "You violated campus rules. Two of them."

My hands clench into fists. "Everyone uses faculty keycards. You could find a dozen students who use copied cards, at least a few faculty who allow it."

"This isn't about other students or faculty. It's about you. And the more serious charge is the financial contribution."

"The money that was supposed to be from my father? Fine, it was my money. So what?"

"We have rules in place, Olivia," the vice provost weighs in. "Not only for tax purposes but for the legitimacy of this organization. Impersonating someone else, even a member of your own family, is a serious violation."

Even if the dean threatened to shut down Stars if I didn't come up with the money?

This place made me who I am. It's where I learned to have dreams of my own, where I dared to become something more than what my family wanted of me.

"What about Stars? And Engineering Society? And Fall Ball committee?"

"We appreciate what you've brought to the student body. Don't worry, the events you care for will continue without you." The dean's tight-lipped smile guts me. "Your transcripts will be finalized and sent to you by mail. We expect you to begin your preparations to leave campus immediately."

Leave campus.

They expect me to move out.

Pack up my life. Say goodbye to my friends, my roommates.

My vision blurs, the blue and burgundy banners on the wall behind the desk blending together.

The recruiting pamphlets say blue is for the ocean and red is the color of leaves in the fall. But the upperclassmen tell the freshmen Russell Red is the color of blood—you go to Russell, play for Russell, cheer for Russell, you're one and the same.

But I'm not one. Not anymore.

"Miss Barclay, security can escort you back to your room. Professor Redmond, if you'll stay a minute longer, we need to discuss the terms for your continued employment."

"Sawyer..." The word comes out strangled.

He's stock-still a few feet away, his dark eyes conflicted.

"I wanted you because I couldn't have you. It wouldn't have worked beyond these walls."

His words from minutes ago in the hallway come back to me.

He didn't mean it, he was only lashing out. He must understand I care about him, but I couldn't drop everything and follow him to New York.

Someone grabs my arm and I jolt. Security entered without me noticing.

"Don't touch her."

Sawyer's words have an undercurrent of threat. The security officer stiffens and releases his grip.

"Olivia..."

Sawyer's voice makes my breath hitch with hope.

Fuck them, I urge.

Fight for me, Sawyer.

Fight for us.

He turns to me, taking my shoulders in his palms.

"...You need to leave. Now."

The words are a blade in my chest.

He's here in this place that's the root of so many wounds. Betrayal by his father, the dean, the school. And he's being offered vindication.

He's the prize and I'm the liability.

The truth of it slams into me and I jerk away to take in the other faculty and administration.

"You say you're here for students, but all you care about is covering up your own mistakes. Russell was a fresh start for me, a place I could figure out who I was. I thought it would be different than all the backstabbing I grew up with. But you do the same thing." The air is thick and heavy, and I struggle against it as I go on. "Instead of calling it manners or taste, you bow to rules and reputation. This place taught me to stand on my own feet, but it wasn't classes. It was you. I guess that's worth two and a half years of tuition."

I shove the hair over my shoulder. "I don't need an escort," I inform the security guard. "I'll walk myself."

"Miss Barclay," the vice provost calls as I'm halfway to the door, her voice softer. "As it's exam week, you can have until the weekend to gather your things and depart campus."

My hand shakes as I yank open the door.

I won't take until the weekend.

I won't even take a day.

2

OLIVIA

"Nope. Nope. Hell no," Emma says.

I stop outside my sister's bedroom door, a cardboard box in my hands. "What's no?"

"All of these things. I don't need to move any of them to the new apartment."

I set the box on her bed, shifting onto the end to stare down at where she's cross-legged on the floor. What looks like the contents of her closet are sorted into three ruthless piles, the largest of which has a sheet of paper with the word DONATE scrawled on it.

"It's downsizing. It's not as we're living under a bridge, Ems."

"You didn't live here at all. You got out." She drops a top into the donate pile. "But now you're back."

Since I was expelled, the winter break has been a blur of empty festivities, a few parties, my parents steering carefully clear of my plans for the new year.

My second day home, my mom commented on my hair and I stared at her with dead eyes until she looked away.

My family has given me a wide berth since.

Kismet trots into the room, spinning a circle in Emma's pile of clothes before heading into the closet.

"If I didn't know better, I'd say you aren't as upset about school as you are about something else." Emma rises and shifts onto the bed next to me, clutching a skirt to her chest. "You haven't said a word for the last two weeks, but if you didn't have some fight with your hottie professor, I don't get why you stare into your coffee and barely eat. So talk to me. I'm your sister."

I made a mistake telling the dean I got money from my dad, giving him Lancaster's money instead. I thought it would help with our project. Instead, it landed me in a pile of trouble bigger than Emma's DONATE stack.

But I'd be lying if I said school was the only source of my dark mood the past two weeks.

The first time Sawyer's number flashed across my screen, I was on the train heading home.

The second time, I was out shopping for Christmas presents with Emma.

The third time, I was baking cookies for a fundraiser.

I stabbed the decline button with flour-covered fingers and tossed my phone in a drawer for the next three days.

There's nothing he can say to make it right.

He risked so much to be with me for months. But he wanted me to drop everything and follow him, and when I couldn't, he decided I wasn't worth it. *We* weren't worth it.

"He wanted me to be someone I wasn't. And when I couldn't, he chose Russell over me."

"I'm sorry, Liv. I'm not letting anyone come and ruin my happiness," Emma says.

Surprise has me shifting off the bed. "You're happy?"

"Yes. Thanks to Trey."

Emma glances to the half-open door, shutting it to a crack. Our parents have been arguing most of the holidays, Mom finally being more vocal about the fact she's upset that Dad screwed us out of the family's money. I'm starting to wonder if they'll last.

"New Year's Eve I said I was going to that party, but I went to his place instead. He planned this whole night for us, with music, and candles... He got vanilla ones by mistake, and his brothers have been giving him shit ever since because their entire place still smells like it." Her lips curve and she tugs on a piece of hair. "I figured it would hurt, or that he'd rush, but he didn't."

The feeling in my chest is gratitude, not envy. "Tell me you're being safe."

"Of course. I don't want to get pregnant young like Mom. Sorry," she goes on at my look.

Emma turns to her pile of clothes, tossing another few garments into the box to donate.

The dog returns, something lightly in her teeth.

"Mr. Snuffles!" My lips twitch.

Emma lifts it gingerly from Kismet's mouth. "God. This thing is old."

"Mom and Dad got that for you when you were two. They wanted to get you this swan, but I told them you'd like the elephant better."

"Its trunk is all smooshed."

"Because you wouldn't let it go."

"What the hell." Emma tosses it into a separate pile.

"Where's your box for things to move?"

"I have a couple by the front door, but Mr. Snuffles can go in there." She nods to a big suitcase in the corner and Kismet paws at the door.

"I'm going to take her out," I tell Emma, heading for the door.

"Liv?" My sister's voice stops me. "I love you. You know that."

I frown at her weird inflection. "I love you too. Didn't think Mr. Snuffles would make you so sentimental."

I grab Kismet's leash and pull on boots.

We walk the entire Upper West Side. It's been covered in snow since New Year's.

I couldn't control what happened at school this fall. Now, I need to figure out a path forward—something I couldn't bring myself to do since returning, but I'll have to square with soon enough.

When I get home, the fresh air has me feeling a bit better.

The second I walk in the door, my mother's voice calls. "Olivia?"

"Yeah." I tug off my scarf, meeting her worried gaze.

"Did you take Emma with you?"

"No. She's packing."

I unclip Kismet's leash and step out of my boots, padding down the hall. Emma's door is open and I lean in.

No sign of her.

"She probably went to hang out with her friends." *Or her boyfriend.*

I start to head back out, but do a double take—not at what's there, but what's missing.

Her huge suitcase.

Worry creeps into my stomach, and I grab my phone and dial her number.

There's no answer.

SAWYER

"You need the foam finger," Daniel calls over the crowd.

I flip up my jacket collar against the cold wind. "I'm not getting a foam finger."

"It's part of the experience."

The experience in question is an NFL game, the stadium packed to bursting with stalwart fans. Every person here is elated to bear witness to today's contest. A team surrounding a team, all because they want to wear the same colors and rejoice or mourn in unison over an athlete they'll never meet toting a ball across an arbitrary line.

"Does the man not know how to attend a football game? My gift to you." Ricardo passes me a huge foam finger from his seat on the other side of Andy and Daniel.

My lip curls and Andy laughs.

When Daniel and the guys insisted I take the extra seat, they claimed it was to take advantage of winter break before school starts next week.

Because I haven't been enjoying my hard-won time off?

On the outside, I might look like I have my shit together, but I got through exams on sheer will. The TAs grading were from the department pool, which was fine until one of them stupidly brought to my attention that a third-year student didn't take her exam and what should he do with her final grade?

Two guesses who that was.

Since getting expelled, Olivia and I haven't spoken. She cleared out of her residence room in record time, then ignored my calls over winter break.

We've never gone this long without talking, and it's driving me insane.

Every time I hear her cheerful instructions to leave a message, I want to punch something. I couldn't bring myself to text her because the conversation we need to have won't happen in pixels.

She's torn up over being forced out of Russell. The way she looked at me in that room still haunts me.

Doesn't she understand that my instinct was to tear through every person there, starting with the dean?

She wanted me to save her.

I am saving you, I wanted to shout in her face.

A woman passes down the row with a bright ballcap and my eyes follow her.

Zander laughs. "You want a purple hat, Redmond?"

"Yeah, I think I do." I need to stretch my legs, plus there's someone who would get a kick out of the souvenir.

On my way out of our seats, I pass a section made up mostly of kids from about Andy's age to high school. Their energy is palpable, their eyes bright with delight.

One of the guys with them files after me toward the inside of the stadium.

"Sweet section for a bunch of kids," I comment.

"It's Big Brothers, Big Sisters. The team donates a group of tickets. Grown-ups get to go for free, which is a bonus, but it's worth it to see the kids so happy."

It's the end of halftime when I get through the line and pay for the overpriced headgear and head back to the game.

Andy points to the cheerleaders. "They're really good!"

"I was never into cheerleaders," Ric says.

"But they're so flexible. *Emotionally* flexible," Zander amends at Daniel's pointed look. "You ever date a girl who could bring her foot up that high?"

"Yeah," I say.

"And how was it?"

She stole my heart and wore it around her neck like her diamond.

"Complicated."

Play resumes but the guys' attention is on me. If this was an excuse for a therapy session, we could've tailgated without the pricey tickets.

"She thinks I turned my back on her and she's not speaking to me." I squint at Daniel through the late afternoon sun.

"I want you to be happy. And if this girl makes you happy...you should try."

"I've tried. Believe me."

"She doesn't want to hear what you're saying, find something new to say." Daniel shakes a foam finger in my face.

"Do that one more time, I'll shove that up your ass."

3

OLIVIA

It's been hours and there's still no word from Emma.

It's possible she went off with friends, but I'm worried she didn't answer my text. And she was acting strange before she left.

"Liv? I love you. You know that."

I've tried calling and texting, even checked some of her favorite places around our neighborhood. Maybe she's more bummed about the move than she let on.

Which doesn't explain the missing suitcase.

When I trudge home and let myself in, I've barely dropped into a chair in the living room when the front door cracks.

"Hello?"

I leap up and run to the hall at Emma's voice.

"Where have you been?"

She's there, beaming, her hair curled and eyes lined and cheeks pink. "At Trey's place. I'm going back there now."

"We were worried about you."

"You don't need to worry anymore." She holds up a hand and a clear stone blinks from her fourth finger. "I'm engaged."

She turns her hand and I grasp it, my stomach falling through the floor.

My baby sister is engaged? Is that possible?

"Why didn't you say anything?"

"You would've tried to talk me out of it."

"Because you're in high school! You have your whole life ahead of you," I gasp.

"He's the one, Liv. I know it! Mom even tried to break us up, but it didn't work. I told you we've been hanging out all break and it's been insanely romantic."

"But...how are you going to finish school?"

"He and his brothers have a place in the Bronx. I can finish from there." My sister's glowing. "You'll love him. He's strong, and passionate, and rough around the edges..."

"Emma?" My mother sweeps in from the kitchen, surveying Emma from head to toe.

Her gaze stops at Emma's hand. She presses her

own hand to her face.

"Mom. You're pale. I think you should sit down..." I grab for her as she slips.

I half help, half carry her to the couch.

"We broke Mom," Emma whispers.

"I had nothing to do with it. Go to the kitchen and get me a damp towel. If you can do that without causing any more drama."

She starts that way, her shoulders slumping.

Feeling like an asshole, I turn to call after her. "Tell me he at least got down on one knee."

She turns back and her lips twitch. "He did."

***

I'm in bed that night after she's gone off with her boyfriend.

Fiancé.

Whatever he is this week.

Mom was inconsolable, even with Dad to comfort her.

Emma promised I could meet Trey soon. When she showed me pictures from the proposal, her beaming and a too-good-looking guy with wicked eyes and straight teeth, a pang hit me in the stomach.

Not because I envied her, but because I had no

idea this was going on and I wish she'd confided in me.

Why didn't she? Have I been that caught up in my own business I haven't been paying enough attention to my sister?

"Come to New York with me."

Sawyer didn't ask me to marry him, but he asked me to take a chance on him.

If I had, would I be lying next to him in some Midtown condo, his body warming mine, instead of here alone, willing my stupid heart to stop throbbing?

I roll over for the thousandth time. Despite the cool air in my bedroom, I'm hot everywhere. My tank top and shorts feel like a snowsuit.

I haven't been touched in weeks, but my body hasn't gotten the message that physical satisfaction is off the priority list.

There's no reason it has to be just because the rest of my life is imploding.

As I shift in bed and slip a hand down my stomach, my phone vibrates on my pillow in the dark.

Repentant Asshole: I have something you've been missing.

. . .

I shoot upright.

Sawyer.

We haven't talked since before the break. He *cannot* be trying to flirt with me right now.

Then again, this is the man who fingered me against his car in the middle of his driveway. Subtlety isn't his strong suit.

Traitorous heat floods my body, settling between my thighs.

Not happening.

I'm not sure if I'm telling him or myself.

My fingers fly over the keyboard, writing and deleting words.

You can't be serious. You think you can drop some dirty talk and I'll come running...

I pause my typing as an image comes through.

It's a piece of tape with my name in Lancaster's handwriting.

A second photo is of the fish tank.

The breath whooshes out, an embarrassed flush crawling up my cheeks.

He wasn't sexting me.

But then what does he mean...

A swell of emotion lodges in my throat.

Liv: Lancaster left me his fish?

. . .

He kept this from me.

Why?

I zoom in on the picture. Half a dozen fish are visible, including the black ghost knife fish.

Liv: You've been feeding them.

Repentant Asshole: Once or twice.

My gasp is audible. As if he hears it, he texts back.

Repentant Asshole: Yes, I'm feeding them. The fish are fine.

Repentant Asshole: How are you?

It takes a moment to realize I answered his text. Before even deciding I was going to.

. . .

Liv: Was this your plan? Hold the fish ransom so I'd talk to you?

Dots appear immediately.

Repentant Asshole: That doesn't sound like me.

I snort, incredulous.

Liv: Don't act offended. You stole my underwear the first time in your office.

Repentant Asshole: You moaned when I dragged them off you.

My breath catches.

It's so easy to slip into familiar banter with this man. To pretend the last few weeks never happened, that I could hop on the train and be back in his arms in two hours, trading smiles and filthy promises and shutting out the world.

. . .

Repentant Asshole: And that was the second time in my office.

Repentant Asshole: The first time you showed up with paint on your arm and your perfect mouth in this tight little line because you weren't taking no for an answer.

I should hate him, but I can't.

I love him too much.

I shift in bed, the soft sheets feeling rough against my back as I turn over and stare up at the phone screen.

Repentant Asshole: I'm bringing you the fish.

The idea of Sawyer here makes my heart race.

His dark, hungry gaze.

Him climbing over me in my queen bed, the canopy over top, where Adam and I hooked up once senior year when my parents were away.

He wouldn't care what's packed in the boxes, or what my parents are fighting about beyond the door, he'd only care about me.

Liv: Don't. Keep them.

Repentant Asshole: He wanted you to have them.

Liv: Just...keep them for now. Until I figure out what I'm doing.

Repentant Asshole: What are you doing?

Awareness prickles my skin, and I swallow.

Liv: Lying in bed.

Repentant Asshole: I meant in New York.

. . .

Gah. Of course that's what he meant.

I tell the throbbing between my thighs to cease and desist.

Liv: I'm looking into schools. I'm a year and a half short of graduating, so I'd need to transfer my credits.

Repentant Asshole: Don't get ahead of yourself.

Irritation rises up, slicing through the haze of arousal.

Liv: I get that you picked Russell over me, but you think I should give up on a degree altogether? That's cold, Professor.

Repentant Asshole: Not what I meant. And if you think I picked Russell over you, you're not as smart as I thought you were.

. . .

With everything that went down today, my emotions are all over the place. I don't trust myself and I sure as hell don't trust him.

Liv: I need to sleep. Thanks for not killing my fish.

I drop back against the pillow and toss the phone to the carpet next to my bed. The phone's screen is a bright outline until it finally clicks off.

I shut my eyes for a minute.

Two.

Ten.

Sleep won't come.

Because I'm a glutton for punishment and talking to him reminds me how much I miss his company, I shift off the edge of my bed and reach for the phone.

Liv: How's the team?

I hold my breath, thinking he's not going to answer.

One minute later, he does.

.   .   .

Repentant Asshole: Adam's not the sharpest pencil in the box.

Repentant Asshole: Still not sure how you dated him for three years.

My mouth twitches.

Liv: We grew up together. He was cute.

Repentant Asshole: Is that why you dated me?

The hairs on my neck lift.

Liv: We never dated.

Repentant Asshole: What would you call it?

The most incredible whirlwind.

Feeling alive for the first time.

Riding the edge of a cliff and not caring whether I stayed on top or fell over, as long as I was with you.

Liv: A mistake.

It's not true, but I don't take it back. If I give Sawyer an inch, he'll strip away my walls and do whatever he wants with what he finds inside.

Repentant Asshole: That's bullshit and you know it.

I roll onto my back and shut my eyes.

I clutch the phone to my chest, imagining I can feel him instead. His strong shoulders and lean hips and firm lips that torment every inch of me.

It's seconds or minutes before my phone vibrates again.

**Repentant Asshole: If you need a reference for school, I'll get you one. I'll always give you what

you need.

I'll always give you what you need.

I stare at the pixels in black and white on my phone.

Sawyer's talking about school, but the sudden arousal heating my body didn't get the memo.

The fact that he turned me into a woman who's used to regular orgasms and great sex doesn't have to be a bad thing.

It doesn't have to be personal. He doesn't have to know.

I'm in control.

I switch a couple of settings to activate voice-to-text.

My fingers slip down to caress my breast, my nipple already hard.

"You think you know what that is?" I murmur, quiet enough my voice doesn't reach my closed door not to mention my parents' room down the hall.

The phone converts it to text, and sends it off at the touch of a button.

Repentant Asshole: Tell me what you want and it's yours.

·   ·   ·

My fingers are under my panties, teasing. My hips arch up off the bed.

I'll always give you what you need.

Tell me what you want and it's yours.

My eyes drift closed as I stroke deeper, my thumb rolling over my clit and my fingers sliding lower.

Need courses through me, the pulse of pleasure tugging all the way from my breasts to where I'm touching myself.

"Yes," I whisper.

Repentant Asshole: Or I could just tell you what you need.

I picture Sawyer on his elbows over me, all dark intensity and warm mirth.

He nudges my thighs wider.

He's fingering me, his dark eyes locked on mine and promising all kinds of sins. He strokes long and slow, hitting me in that spot along my front wall that makes me hiss.

"Oh God, don't stop."

His thumb presses down on my clit, and he

lowers his dirty mouth to my body, tracing his lips along the curve of my breast before sucking so hard on my nipple that my toes cramp.

I drop the phone on the bed and plunge two fingers where I'm soaked and aching.

When the climax rips through me, it's the hardest I've come in weeks. Tremors wrack my body for ages.

Eventually, the buzz of the phone makes me crack open an eye I didn't realize was shut.

There are no new texts

But there is a voice message.

My stomach tightens.

I hit play and Sawyer's growl fills my ears.

"If I'd known you were going to get off to this, I would've been more direct."

He heard me.

Somehow, the phone got my moans and comments.

Shit.

Another message appears. My sweat-damp hair sticks to my forehead, my finger hovering over the play button before I hit it.

"You might not want to hear what I have to say, but hear this, Cherry... You can run anywhere. We both know when you moan, it's still my name on your lips. When you come, it's still my cock you feel."

4

____

OLIVIA

I wake up to the sound of arguing in the hall, still groggy after drifting in and out of sweat-soaked dreams all night.

Last night was a minor setback.

Yes, it was sweet that he took care of the fish.

My fish.

But that doesn't change the reality that he was right about one thing...

Our relationship wasn't meant to survive outside of Russell.

And future conversations about fish or exes or orgasms are strictly off the table.

Padding to the door, I crack it open.

"There she is!" Jules calls from the front door.

Kat ducks under my mom's arm, taking in my pajamas. "You're not dressed for this."

"What's this?"

"A kidnapping. We're going to the Brooklyn Flea Market, and tonight we have tickets for Drunk Shakespeare."

My heart lifts. "Give me fifteen minutes."

I go back into my room to get ready. In record time, I'm back in the hallway and dressed for the day.

"This place would make a great laser tag setup." Jules peers around the boxes stacked everywhere as I pull my jacket on.

"Moving truck comes tomorrow. I'm glad you guys are here."

"You might not be in a second," Jules says cryptically as we head outside.

There's a car parked on the road, and in the back, a head bobs.

My feet stop. "What the…"

The door opens, and a redhead shifts out eyeing me warily.

"Madison? You guys brought Madison?!"

There's a long list of people I'm not excited to see right now, and she's near the top of it.

We might be on better terms than we were at the beginning of the semester, but she did nothing to speak up for me when it was clear the guys wanted to kick me off the team. She practically waved goodbye with a smile on her face.

Kat slides between us. "She was desperate. There was begging. It wasn't pretty."

I fold my arms and cut a look over her shoulder.

Madison holds out a coffee. "We need to talk."

I take it from her. "Not talking."

"Then you can listen. Get in the car."

The four of us head to Brooklyn, me and Madison in the back. It's the most awkward group in history.

"The team is in trouble without you," Madison says as we start for the flea market.

"It hasn't been the best holiday for me either."

In my limited researching of schools, I found out Columbia wouldn't admit me until at least the fall, which means I have the winter, spring, and summer before I could get in anywhere else—even with good grades and glowing references.

Probably from guys I haven't fucked.

"I went to see the dean last week. And he was creepy."

Jules turns to listen. This must've been what she told my roommates to make them bring her.

"What do you mean creepy?"

"Just weird. I needed a signature on some forms for school, and he was asking all kinds of questions. Told me I had a bright future. But in that icky way."

On the weekend, the traffic is relatively light, but it's still New York. I wish this car could move faster.

"If you want to commiserate, I'm here. But I'm not sure what else I can do."

"Come back to Russell, help with the team."

Her suggestion floors me.

"I can't. Do you not remember? It was a whole big thing where Adam caught me, and Sawyer faced this panel, and that's what you guys wanted."

They spoke up for Professor Redmond, and not a word for me.

"This isn't about your degree, it's about Stars. The biggest competition in the country."

It's one more sharp pain in my gut that I had to leave school, my friends, and the contest I put everything into. "I can't come back. I'm working on getting my courses transferred into Columbia, or somewhere else."

"That will take months. What're you going to do first?"

"Take a break?" Kat weighs in. "Relax a hot second? You have friends from high school you could hang with. Fly out to Tahoe, tell the world to fuck off for a while. Our girl's never done that in her life."

"And she's not about to start."

Madison shoves her hair over her shoulder, turning to face me. "If we win this competition, the money will be split three ways. A million dollars. I'll give you half my share."

More than a hundred and fifty thousand dollars.

That would pay for me to finish school and get a fresh start anywhere I want, without my parents' involvement.

But that would mean moving back to Russell.

Seeing Sawyer.

"No."

The car slides to a stop at a traffic light, and Madison's eyes round. "What do you mean no?"

"Exactly what I said. I'm not going to drop my life and rush to help. And it's not like I even can. I'd have nowhere to live—"

"You could move back into our place," Jules chimes.

"Thanks, but the administration would lose their shit if they found out you were hiding me. I won't put you guys at risk. There's nothing for me at Russell anymore. No one."

Madison drops back in her seat, quiet.

Kat turns around, looking between me and Madison. "I guess this is going to be a long day, huh?"

"This is it," Mom says, eyeing up the new apartment with suspicion.

The boxes are stacked in our new place. Kismet is already wearing a path in the carpet, uneasy with the new environment.

I head to the second of three bedrooms. "Not that one," Dad calls. "That's my office."

"Hard to imagine you'd need it. Surely you can run this family into the ground from the sofa."

Good one, Mom.

I carry my bag and try the next door.

The third bedroom is small, and there are already boxes labeled "guest room" piled as high as the window on one side of the double bed.

I locate the final box I packed yesterday and rip off the tape. The table lamp on top is my newest possession, made out of a huge conch shell that's a creamy white on the outside and bright, fresh coral within. Whoever made it found a shade nearly the same color as the outside of the shell.

I bought it at Kat and Jules' prodding at the flea market yesterday, and I set it on the nightstand and search for an outlet.

"Olivia, you're not keeping that. It's heinous." My mom's voice comes from the door.

"It's cute." I lower my voice as she steps inside.

"How bad are things with Dad's work? Now that we've moved, I mean."

She sits on the bed next to me. "Your father made poor decisions, and those last a lifetime."

I spend the rest of the afternoon unpacking and trying not to think about it being the first day back at school.

Students exchanging holiday and New Year's stories.

My roommates grabbing lunch at the UC.

Sawyer looking gorgeous at the front of his class.

I'm tempted to pull up the R.U. Down website and scan through the feeds for posts about extracurriculars, how the school sports teams are doing, or the latest Kappa scandal.

Instead, I toss my phone in the drawer.

It's late when I dig it back out to find three notifications of missed calls, and one voicemail.

When I see who it's from, my stomach drops. In all the chaos, I managed to forget one of my few remaining responsibilities.

I hit a contact on my phone.

"Hello?" A female voice answers.

"Theresa? I'm so sorry I didn't show up to teach class. It's been insane here, but I know that's not an excuse."

I brace myself for her wrath. My former dance

teachers would have chewed me out for being late, not to mention missing a class I was teaching.

But Theresa just chuckles. "The guppies missed you."

My stomach relaxes a bit. Picturing their excited faces makes me happy and sad at once. "And I miss them. But I won't be coming back."

"Why not?"

I pick at the tape on the last remaining box. "I made a mistake that got me kicked out of Russell."

If I expect her to gasp or demand an explanation, she does neither.

"Russell. Not Elmwood."

"Technically."

"So tell me again why you can't teach?"

Teaching was one of the best parts of last semester. Money aside, it calmed me down and made me feel like I could share my experience and love of dance.

"I would love to teach for you." There's little to no chance I'll get into classes at a new college before at least the summer, so it's not as if I'd be putting off my education. "But I don't have anywhere to live."

"I have a room over the studio. It's not fancy, but I could rent it to you. And you can take on more hours teaching if you need the money."

I pull out a rose-colored pillow from the box,

picking at the seam. Madison's offer drifts back through my mind.

If I returned to Elmwood, maybe, just maybe, I would take her up on it. If we win, the money would be great, and we'd have accomplished something real.

Shouting comes from outside my room, my mother's voice. This time, my father shouts back.

I take a breath. "It sounds perfect."

5

OLIVIA

"The stairs are creaky, like any old house. Watch your step."

Theresa holds the door at the top and I follow her inside, suitcase in tow.

To the left is a hallway down to the upstairs studio. She opens the door on the right to reveal a bright kitchen and living area.

"I'm over there." She nods to another door inside this section of the house. "We're separated from the upstairs studio by that partition wall."

She walks me across the kitchen to a door. The room itself is small, with a bed, a dresser, and a desk wedged in one corner.

"The way you described it, I thought this would be a lot less...furnished."

"Well, when you decided to come, I added a few

things.”

My chest squeezes. “Thank you.”

“Now, rules. There aren’t many. You can pay rent from your wages for teaching. There’s a microwave and mini fridge here”—she points to a corner—”but if you need to use the kitchen, that’s fine. In addition to the stairs, there’s a fire escape out the back.”

I cross to the other side of the room where a large window occupies most of the wall.

“In terms of visitors, I would prefer you didn’t have men overnight. With Velvet, I see enough during the night. I don’t need to wake up to one in my kitchen at four AM if you know what I mean.”

“What if I’m into women?” I deadpan.

“That’s fine. Tear the roof off, honey.”

The laugh bubbles up. “Got it. No men.”

“Theresa!” comes a voice behind us, and I jump.

“Is someone else here?”

“Very important.” She crooks a finger and I follow her out to the kitchen and dining area. In the corner of the dining room is a covered cage, and she tugs the fabric off to reveal a bright green bird the length of my forearm. “This is Monty.”

“Hi, Monty.”

“He’s named after my ex-husband.”

“And he talks?”

“Occasionally. But the words he knows are few

and far between, and he hasn't been speaking much lately. He's been in a bit of a mood."

I feel you, Monty.

She walks me back to my room. On the way I catch sight of a photo on the wall of ballet dancers. At first I think it's a memory from some production she attended, but then I notice the face of one of the principal dancers.

"Is that you?"

She smiles. "It is. I danced with the San Francisco Ballet."

"Wow. I had no idea."

"I still sneak into the studio if I can't sleep, or I'm up early. You can use it too, you know."

I look past her down the stairs. "I'm not a dancer anymore."

"You're always a dancer."

After she leaves, I unpack my suitcase, splitting clothes between the narrow closet and dresser, and put my notebook computer on the desk to charge.

I set the lamp I bought this past weekend on the bedside table. When I flick it on, it casts a warm glow over the bedspread and worn hardwood floor that brings a smile to my lips.

Tomorrow I need to teach dance for three hours instead of the usual one, and I'll meet the team in lab at the time Madison suggested when I called to let her know I was coming back.

Now, I change my clothes and pull on tights and a leotard. Classes are wrapping up for the day and I head down the stairs after the last group of senior girls are finished.

I hit the switch in the studio, and the lights flicker on one row at a time.

My feet pad across the sprung wood floors, and I feel it in my heels, the balls of my feet, every one of my toes.

I cross to the sound system and flip through the music, landing on a Prince track. It comes on too loud, and I turn it down so Theresa doesn't get blasted upstairs.

On a Tuesday night, the parking lot is empty, the streetlights guarding the quiet road.

I take my spot at the bar and start to work.

Warming up with pliés and developpés.

Legs, hips, feet, core, shoulders, arms.

In the fall I worked on all of it with the kids, but never myself.

It feels good.

It feels healing.

The track changes once, twice, before I move to the corner of the room.

The first series of chassés and jetés is restrained, but each pass is more open than the last.

Machines are fascinating, but they're not as incredible as the engineering of living things. Human beings, flesh and blood and bone. Strength and weakness. Perfection and flaws.

There's only Prince in my ears, life in my limbs.

When I stop next to the window, headlights in the small parking lot make me tense.

The truck is familiar, and I peer through the glass, my heart thudding.

I cross to the front door, unlocking it and leaning out. "Daniel?"

He turns around and makes his way toward me, sheepish. "I was dropping off a check." He gestures to the locked dropbox by the door. "I thought that was you, but I figured I must have been wrong. Because you left town," he goes on at my silence.

I wrap my bare arms around me against the cold. "It would be better if you didn't tell Sawyer I'm back."

"He doesn't know?" Daniel's eyes narrow.

I go to shove a hand through my hair, then realize it's pinned up in a bun. "I got here and...I need a couple of days."

He doesn't answer but starts back toward his truck.

"Daniel!" I call. "Please?"

He turns back and watches me. "When we were kids, he was a mutt with a bone, impulsive and tenacious and I gave him shit for it. But when my wife got sick, she had certain wishes that it destroyed me to grant her." Daniel grimaces, his pain etched plainly on his face. "Her parents held it against me, but Sawyer had my back. He fought like a dog for me and for Andy when I couldn't."

Imagining Sawyer going to war for his friend makes my heart beat faster. "I'm glad he defended you. He didn't defend me."

I don't know why I'm telling Daniel, except that it's a weight on my chest that's been pressing for weeks. "The university expelled me, Daniel, and he just stood there and didn't do a thing. The man who's always said and done exactly what he wants, no matter the consequences—"

"Then that must have been hell for him. Because he cares about you more than he's ever cared about anything." Daniel jerks open the door. "Maybe you're right. It's better he doesn't know you're back."

His truck peels out of the lot and I'm left staring after him long after my teeth start to chatter from the cold.

6

SAWYER

"You can't be serious. The entire semester?" Tate barks in my ear as I cross the walkway from my car to the house.

"Looks that way," I inform my future business partner.

During exams, I called Tate to say I'd accepted a contract extension and we would have to defer our plans another few months. He's not happy about it.

"Two months ago, you were planning your escape," he says, suspicious.

"I need to see a few things through."

"Listen. When I said last summer that our agreement was contingent upon you keeping your nose clean for a year, I didn't expect you to oblige me to the day."

"Evidently I'm the obliging sort," I deadpan.

"Bullshit. You're taking this responsibility seriously. Is this about Stars?"

In a way.

It was mere luck he didn't hear about Olivia the end of last semester. But evidently whatever gossip there was got shut down quickly.

"You're committed to those kids," he goes on. "It's admirable. Still, this competition might be a spectacle, but it's for the students. It will hardly change the trajectory of your career. If it comes down to it, I expect your loyalty to lie with our future."

"You sound rather agitated. Have you had your blood pressure checked lately?"

"It's quite normal, thank you, Dr. Redmond." His wry response has my mouth twitching. "But I've secured us a workspace. And at the end of this semester, we need to move on this. Understood?"

"Yeah. And thanks for moving it forward," I add. There might have been no love lost between us when I was at the old company, but Tate's been decent since I proposed this new partnership.

I click off and adjust the computer bag on my shoulder.

The first week of winter term has been a rush of students scrambling to adjust schedules, finding new classrooms and routines.

Now, my stomach is rumbling. I skipped lunch in my efforts to review the timing of my midterm instead of thinking that the student in my third-year class occupying the seat that Olivia used to sit in is blonde, not brunette.

I take the stairs up the porch I built with my own hands. The healthy boards offer not so much as a creak beneath my feet. Evidently the realtor made it here to take down the SOLD sign.

Daniel's truck pulls into the driveway across the road. As he gets out, I wave, and he slams the door.

I frown as I watch him pace toward the house, then away from it. Halfway to the porch again, he pulls up.

"You good?" I call.

He shoves a hand through his hair. "You, ah... you want to pick Andy up after dance?"

I tuck my phone in my pocket. "I was going to grab takeout, but I can if you need me to."

My friend folds his arms. "Yeah. Thanks."

Then he turns and ducks into his house.

Well, that was fucking weird.

An hour later, I'm parked in front of the dance studio and holding the door for one of the moms. Jean—at least I think that's her name—is smiling and flirting, and I'm about to excuse myself the second Andy's free.

But when I look towards the studio, every muscle in me goes tight.

Olivia crosses the floor, hair pinned up and mouth curved in a conversation with her stumbling kids.

I haven't laid eyes on her in almost three weeks, and it's a physical relief to see her.

This is why Daniel wanted me to come.

When she spots me, her lips part and her pretty eyes blink, as if she's every bit as affected as I am.

Last week I was tired of her blowing me off, so I texted her about the fish. Got more than I bargained for.

I thought her breathy moans were a joke.

But when I realized she was touching herself, a beast inside me broke free of its chains, feral and triumphant.

"Uncle Sawyer!" Andy's on me, grabbing at my jeans.

"Hey, Andy. Your dad asked me to come get you."

"Can we go to McDonald's for dinner?"

"I think your dad's got something planned."

"Better than chicken nuggets?" He's doubtful, and I sigh.

"I'm not going to lie to you. We both know there's nothing better than chicken nuggets."

"So we can go!" He laughs.

"That's above my paygrade, kid. You'll have to take it up with him." I lean in. "But next time, it's nuggets all around."

Olivia crosses to us and my chest constricts as I get a hit of her light, floral scent.

"So I was going to find out you were here...when I ran into you at CVS buying chips and lube?" I ask under my breath.

She smiles and waves at some other kids who leave, ignoring my question.

It's one thing for us not to talk every day. Pretty big difference from her failing to mention she's back in the same town.

Daniel's kid finishes pulling on his boots and jacket.

"I have to take Andy home," I decide. "Then we'll get dinner. You need to eat."

"Sawyer—"

"Not asking."

Her eyes flash as if she's going to argue with me but thinks better of it in front of all these kids. Finally, she nods.

My gaze tears away from Olivia to Andy. "Let's go."

Twenty minutes later I'm back, in record time. Don't even have a chance to chew out Daniel.

Olivia's still wearing her tights and leotard with a

skirt and denim jacket overtop as I stop the car in front of the studio. It's already dark, and the parking lot lights illuminate the drizzle coming down.

When she shifts into the passenger side, reaching for the seat belt, her scent hits me again. It's so much better on her than on my pillowcase.

I put the car in gear and pull out into the street before asking, "When did you get back?"

"A couple days ago."

"And you're living..."

"Over the studio. Theresa is renting me a room. It's nice," she goes on as I navigate us to the other side of town. "Small, but cute."

I pull up in front of the diner. We both get out and I put a hand on her lower back as we head inside.

Habit.

Inside, it's warm and dry and nearly empty. There's a group of kids, probably high school, at one end, plus a couple of truckers.

"I haven't been to this place since orientation week," she murmurs, shrugging off her jacket and grabbing a menu in front of her as we slide into opposite sides of a booth.

If I'm going to get her to talk, it's going to take strategy, I realize. Not brute force.

"Before I was adopted it was the one restaurant I

went to." Her gaze cuts to mine, surprised. "They had a two-dollar breakfast special. I got breakfast, no matter what time of day it was."

"All about the hashbrowns?"

"Mostly the ketchup."

Her lips twitch. "You can eat ketchup on other foods. Macaroni. Fries."

"Nah. It's a breakfast food. I will fight anyone who says it isn't."

She rolls her eyes. The familiarity hits me in the gut.

"What can I get you?" The waitress appears, sharp eyes surveying us over her notepad.

Olivia orders soda and a salad, and I get a coffee and breakfast.

Once the woman bustles off with our orders I lean in. "So you're gonna teach ballet in a college town the rest of your life?"

She folds her arms. "Theresa did."

"She also runs a strip club."

"There could be room for two in Elmwood." Her brow arches. "All I know is I'm not getting back into Russell."

It's clipped, her tone, as if she won't let herself hope for it. It's one thing for me to be cynical, but I can't stand it in her.

"Don't say that."

"Why not? I haven't launched a campaign. Have you?" Her lips curve but every muscle in my body is tight.

I don't want to get her hopes up by telling her about the research I've been doing, the files I've been saving and committees I've been stalking.

"There a reason you didn't return a single one of my calls over break?"

Her smile fades. "There was nothing to say. The committee asked you to stay and told me to leave. And you didn't say a word in my defense."

The frustration rises up, sharp and acrid. "Because you chose that moment to act like you're twenty for once—terrible timing, by the way—and declare your independence in a giant fuck-you speech to the administration."

I wanted to burn everything and everyone for her, but that would have guaranteed her exile was permanent.

Instead, when the committee offered to extend my teaching position, I accepted. Even let the real estate deal on my dad's house fall through. It will be difficult for me to have her expulsion overturned as faculty, but it would be impossible if I wasn't with the school anymore.

But she's watching me like she can not only see my thoughts, but deeper. Into my soul. "I'll admit I was emotional," she starts. "But it felt like the second they opened their arms to you, you chose them over me—"

"You did the same thing," I interrupt.

"I didn't..." she starts, her eyes widening.

"Yeah, you did."

When I asked her to come to New York, she passed. The difference is, I'm used to being second choice. I didn't expect it from her, though, which is why the last few weeks have been agony.

"And I'm not saying you shouldn't have, or that it was wrong. But clearly I'm not the only one ready to tattoo the Russell emblem on my ass."

We're still staring at each other when our food arrives.

Finally, Olivia passes me the ketchup and picks up her fork, stabbing a piece of lettuce.

"Tell me that when Madison and the others fought for you, it didn't feel good." Another piece is speared after the first. Then another. "After the way you were forced out last time, I can understand you not wanting to be forced out. Just be honest about it."

She finally puts her fork in her mouth and chews.

"That's not fair, Olivia."

She swallows, reaching for her soda. "None of this is."

The music in the background is soft rock from

the nineties. With the rain coming down on the window, it feels like we're in our own world.

Cars in the parking lot come and go.

Eventually, we start talking again.

Safe things.

I tell her how Andy's started learning about fish. She talks about her parents' move out of their townhouse into an apartment. I talk about the team, and teaching.

We catch up as our meals slowly disappear.

So does the tension in the air.

It's as if neither of us can maintain a standoff. It's not an equilibrium that can be preserved between us.

I can't be around her and not talk to her, push her, wonder what she's thinking.

Never occurred to me it went both ways.

"My sister got engaged to this biker," she offers. "Emma's still in high school, but she says she's in love with this guy and knows he's the one. It's insane. How could she do that? Not to mention bring that news home."

"She probably felt like she could because you've got her back."

Her eyes soften. "It's still crazy. You can't throw away everything you've worked for, everything in your past and start over."

"Can't you?" I study her over the rim of my coffee mug.

She wraps her arms around herself and I'm a heartbeat away from offering her my jacket when she goes on.

"Emma thinks she's free of Mom, but what if all she's doing is what some guy wants instead? She escaped from my parents and had her first taste of the real world. But trying to please other people is a hard habit to kick. So he asks her, and she says yes because even though she has doubts, she's caught up and she can make him happy that way. Or she thinks she can. But is anything better? Is she really free?"

The earnestness hits me in the gut.

She's not talking about her sister. Not really.

The bell over the door sounds. A pack of kids, not much older than I was when I used to come here, tumble inside. They're in sweatshirts too thin for the cold, their laughter loud and their grins shallow.

I came here to get her to admit what she's really doing back in Elmwood. But it's easy to demand and to take.

Harder to listen and to give.

I want to reach over and trap her hands between mine, to say, *You are what I want, Cherry.*

You don't have to try.

I shift back in my seat. "When my mom died, it

was because she chose to. She struggled with substance abuse, something I didn't get until much later. But life was too much. Her past was too much. She looked me in the eyes, and then she left."

I've never told anyone that. Daniel knows because he overheard my dad having a conversation with my social worker. But I've never said it.

Olivia covers her mouth with her hand. "I'm so sorry. I didn't know your mom, but it has nothing to do with you being enough. You were a child. You were perfect."

My lips twitch. "You might not have thought so if you knew me then. I started building things to keep my brain busy, to feel like I had control over something. Anything. My first foster home there was always overflowing garbage cans, so I took some wood and bins from their garage and built a composting system."

"That sounds amazing."

"I was nine and it was terrible. I was labeled as destructive without respect for property. I bounced around a couple of places before Lancaster adopted me. He wanted me to read all the time, but I wanted to make things. He got frustrated." I thought it would be hard to talk about, but it's not. Like someone else's history as opposed to mine. "I still don't know why he took me in at all."

"Does it matter?"

"Yeah. Yeah, it matters. Because if I knew, I could make sense of why he was such a prick."

To me and not to everyone else, I don't add.

But I wonder if she knows what I mean when her eyes work back and forth across mine. "I like who you are, Sawyer Redmond."

It's not "I need you, Sawyer." Or even, "I want you." But the words carve themselves into my heart.

The feelings of rejection and loneliness and grief from back then are miles away; all I feel is the promise of her warmth, her understanding here in this place with plastic placemats and rain sheeting the windows.

"Dessert?" I ask when we're done.

"What time is it?" she asks, looking at my watch.

"Nine."

We've been here almost two hours. I don't want to see her go.

"I should be getting back. I told Theresa we'd go over my teaching schedule."

We shift out of the booth and head up to the counter. We both reach for our wallets to pay, and our hands brush.

"I've got it," I murmur.

"Thanks."

Being here with her reminds me of all the good things between us.

But I can't let her go without pressing a little.

My hand on hers, I tuck her wallet back in her bag. "Olivia...why did you come back?"

I know what I want her to say, but I'm trying to keep an open mind. There are plenty of reasons she might be here—she misses her friends, she wants to try to get back into school, she needs a break from her parents' toxic environment.

She chews her lip. I'd buy her dinner every night if she'd let me do the same.

"For the Stars team. Madison came to my door and said it's not going well. She wants me to come back."

Her answer has me blinking. "Excuse me?" I hand my card to the cashier without looking at the bill. "But you're not a student."

"So I can't officially help. It might violate the actual rules, but not the spirit of them."

"And you said 'no problem'?!" I'm the king of bad ideas, but this one puts mine to shame. "Olivia, this could threaten any chance of you being readmitted. Not to mention they were assholes to you. Please tell me I didn't teach you to bend the rules only to put yourself in harm's way with no chance of getting repaid," I snap.

"It's not no chance. It's the chance I have." Her eyes flash, fire rising up immediately. "Madison promised if the team wins, she'll give me half her share of the money."

I shove my card and the receipt in my pocket as we walk to the front doors.

She's here for money.

She wouldn't change her mind for me, but she'll do it for a few dollars.

The rain's gotten heavier, coming down in massive sheets that would guarantee us getting drenched between here and the car.

"Bad timing," she murmurs, her face nearly pressed to the glass next to mine.

"Wait it out. I don't want you getting soaked."

"It's fine."

I catch her arm. "I won't have you drown on my watch."

She sucks her lower lip between her teeth again. "Why can't you let me look after myself?"

We're inches apart, without the safety of the table to keep me off her.

Because I can look after you so much better.

Her dark lashes are at half-mast when her gaze drops to my mouth.

Fuck, I want to kiss her.

I'd imprint her lips with mine, hard enough she

can't ignore me, soft enough she'll be remembering every night she's in bed alone.

I'd memorize her sharp inhale, that sound that perfectly captures what we are, what she does to me every damn time.

Surprise.

Relief.

Life.

She rips her gaze from mine to look outside.

"It's not letting up. Let's make a run for it."

7

OLIVIA

I agreed to dinner because I had to tell him about the team—he'd find out sooner or later anyway.

But Daniel's words about how hard it must have been for Sawyer not to defend me when I was expelled have been running through my mind all day.

Hearing his voice, looking into his gorgeous dark eyes, itching to thread my fingers in his hair, is the most exquisite torture.

"You chose them over me."

"You did the same."

His confession about his mom rocked me. He's spent his life trying to protect himself from being hurt, believing he's never going to have love because everyone leaves him.

His mom physically. His dad emotionally, by denying him care and attention.

You haven't exactly been the exception to the rule, a voice in my head points out.

That's why I burst through the door and out into the rain.

My feet splash in puddles as I run through the parking lot, dodging the "no idling" sign.

When I make it to the Mercedes, I round to the passenger door. "Hurry!"

He fumbles for his keys, the locks popping open at last. I dive inside and slam the door after me.

"Guess I got my shower after class," I pant, feeling my soaked hair and jean jacket. Rain pelts the roof, staccato plinks like bullets surrounding us.

He hits the engine, the Mercedes purring to life. "If you think that gets you out of talking about that bomb you just dropped, you're wrong."

"Nothing to talk about. You said yourself the team needs help. Something about Adam and pencils," I remind him.

"It's my decision."

"Really? You're not my supervisor. You're not my professor. You're not my boyfriend."

"I'm your mistake?" Sawyer asks.

He turns toward me, raindrops clinging distractingly to his nose and lips.

I'm trapped in his gaze, his presence, his scent that fills the car.

"If this is how you look at your mistakes," he breathes, shoving the wet hair from his face, "I'll gladly be the last mistake you ever make."

My heart stops.

He's not making this easy.

Of course he's not.

When my teeth begin to chatter, he curses and rummages in the back seat and produces a sweatshirt. "Here. It's clean, and it even matches your eyes."

My stomach tightens as I take it.

I start to strip off my jacket and top, elbows bumping the window as I maneuver in the interior.

Damn him and his contradictions.

He's ruthless and sweet.

Reckless and thoughtful.

Careless and caring.

And every time I catch a glimpse of how good he can be, it makes me not want to give up on him.

On us.

"Are you stuck?" he asks seconds later while I'm wrestling with the fabric.

"No."

The smug asshole actually laughs, a deep rumble that warms me all over.

He reaches over to help, dragging the damp fabric off my head.

Light from the parking lot halogens barely cuts through the downpour of rain on the windshield, leaving most of Sawyer's face in darkness.

I don't need light to tell me the shape of his jaw, or the planes of his cheeks, or the bow of his lips.

His fingers brush my cold arms, and goosebumps rise up.

My body goes tight with longing.

"Remember the night we met?" he murmurs. The flare of his nostrils says he's not unaffected either. "You were soaked then, too."

I'll never forget it.

My throat is a desert. "It was vodka, not rain. Super classy."

Rain pelts the car, getting harder. The sound drowns out my thudding heart.

"After all that's happened, do you regret it?" he asks.

"No," I whisper. "I don't regret anything about how we met."

"I do." Sawyer brushes a thumb down my cheek. "I should have made you mine that first night. I should have never let you leave."

The car is too small. The air too thick.

No matter what happened this fall or how he

treated me, there's a flame deep in my chest that burns for him. It can flicker and change colors, burn hotter and cooler with the seasons or my soul, but it won't ever go out.

I stick my arms in the shirt and he tugs it over my head, and his knuckles brush my breasts as he drags the oversized fabric down my body.

Before I can pull back, he twists the sweatshirt in his fist, dragging me over the console and into his lap.

My hands find his chest for balance. He's hard under me, his heart thudding under his strong chest, the wet fabric. When he presses at my lower back, my attention drops to his firm mouth.

The one I've felt on my skin. The one that's brought me pleasure and pain and comfort.

"Sawyer..."

Our lips are a breath apart. Every part of me strains to get closer as the attraction between us flares from a flame into a full-on fire.

I should be pushing him away.

Need to leave.

Can't leave.

My body shivers, from the rain or his closeness.

His hands stroke over my tights under my skirt.

I rock my hips without meaning to.

He's hard under me, but it's not his body but his expression, the need on his face, makes me weak.

Just one taste.

Instead of leaning in to brush his lips over mine, he skates lower, grazing my throat.

I gasp at the feel of him.

It's storming outside, but in here, it's a hurricane. He plunders my skin, greedy, punishing.

My hands shift up his chest, threading in the hair at his nape.

I shift in his lap, pressing against his jeans. He rasps against my mouth and the next second his hands find the crotch of my tights.

He rips them.

Shock ricochets through me.

I rear back, hitting the horn with an elbow. I screech as it blares.

A knocking sound has him cursing and me whipping around to look.

Sawyer buzzes down the window to find our waitress from inside, her hood pulled up over her head.

"No idling," she calls through the half-open window. "I don't mind but the cops have been giving out tickets lately."

"Thanks." I force a smile as Sawyer shuts the window again.

"Well, we don't want to get in trouble," he murmurs against my ear.

Laughter bubbles up from somewhere deep in my chest. When was the last time I laughed?

"That got out of hand."

"Speak for yourself. That was my plan all along."

I pull back to look at him. "Seducing women in cars is your new thing?"

"One woman. One car."

I ignore the way my heart kicks at that comment and shift back over the console into the passenger seat, straightening my clothes.

We can't do this. I'm here to help the team and myself through doing that. Teaching dance might just keep my sanity in the interim.

He can work out whatever his issues are at Russell. But I'm not getting involved again. My situation is precarious enough, and add to that the way he shuts down when people get too close...

Sawyer puts the car in reverse, backing out of the parking spot before turning to face me again.

"Liv." The simple nickname affects me more than any other man's touch ever has. "I gave you space because you were going through something I couldn't fix. Something that was my fault as much as it was yours. But if you think you're going to prance around in my engineering lab and moonlight for my team for the next two months and ignore me while you do it...you're fucking wrong."

It's the last thing he says before pulling out onto the street.

8

———

OLIVIA

My first day back on campus revives old feelings of anticipation and enthusiasm. I grab a coffee at the UC, filing into the lines with students back in classes.

But when I get to the engineering lab, I come crashing back to reality.

My keycard no longer works.

It shouldn't be a surprise, but it still stings—a reminder I'm not welcome here.

Now, I'm sizing up the lock to see if there's any way I can get in when a familiar voice comes from my back.

"Liv? What are you doing here?"

Adam stands a few feet behind me, dressed in a winter coat over jeans, his expression guarded.

"Hi. I hope you have a key."

He's the one who betrayed me most, but I haven't spared many thoughts for him since I left. When I agreed to help the team, I decided to put on the same polite face I used for years jumping through my mother's social hoops.

But he doesn't move, and disbelief rises up.

"Adam? Tell me you knew I was coming back."

"Back? Why the hell are you back?"

"Because I invited her." Madison steps between us. Royce is at her heels.

"You didn't tell him?" I demand. "I thought you three discussed this."

"We didn't." She swipes her card over the door and the light blinks green.

This is not what I signed on for.

But there's nowhere else for me to go, so I follow her inside, holding the door for Adam who's still looking like he's seen an unpleasant ghost.

"What's going on?" Royce asks once we're all inside.

"Madison said you guys needed help."

"We don't," Adam interjects.

"We do." Madison perches on a stool like a queen holding court. "The robot barely floats."

"It's a work in progress," Adam says.

"And since Olivia left, I got to take over liaisons with the dean who's a straight scumbag."

Royce's brows pull together. "You never told me—"

"I shouldn't have to. I want Olivia here."

"Absolutely not," Adam says. "If she stays, I'm going."

Royce snorts. "You can't leave. We have a three-person minimum for the team or we're cut out."

"Then keep Olivia," Adam levels. "Oh wait, you can't because she's not a student."

"Shut up and watch this." Madison opens her computer to a web browser. "This is footage from the competition last year."

The clip shows a huge trade show floor with a stage at one end. Presenting teams are polished, their projects amplified on huge screens at the front of the room.

"Notice anything?" she prompts.

I don't have to say it—they're all professional looking.

"The drama at the end of last semester set us back. We have eight weeks until finals and we don't have a hope in hell at this rate."

"Let's take a look at the robot," I say. "If by the end of the hour you don't want me on the team, I'll leave."

It's a gamble. There's no saying they'll go for it.

And if they don't, I'll be the idiot who came back to town to teach a few dance classes.

No Stars.

No money.

I'll have to face my future, or lack thereof.

But the guys exchange a look and retrieve the robot from its storage place.

"We've built a motor here"—Royce points to it after setting the robot on the lab counter—"but we need to improve buoyancy. At least selectively."

"We want it to be a fish, right?" I ask. "So what if we introduce additional force that will help propel it up and down as well as forward?"

"You want to give it fins."

Madison's mouth twitches. "Team Double V hasn't been the same without you."

"The problem with this team isn't that it didn't have enough chicks. If anything, it's the opposite." Adam folds his arms.

I size him up, from his perfect hair to his expensive sneakers. "You're a lot of things. I never thought a patriarchal asshole was one of them."

He frowns. "I meant because of Redmond, not because you're a woman—"

"Yeah, we know what you think, man. How about less thinking and definitely less talking?" Royce weighs in before turning his back on Adam, who stands rooted to the floor like a statue.

"Does this mean you're coming around to me helping?" I ask Royce under my breath.

"We need all the help we can get. Redmond's been...distracted."

I shiver as I think of last night, Sawyer dragging me into his lap in the Mercedes.

He was focused then.

I shake it off and turn to Madison. "You remember Aliya, whose panel we were on? I want you to watch this video I found of one of their projects. I think we could use similar design principles."

I show them the video and that clinches it—Royce is all in.

We come up with a list of things to work on over the next few weeks, and when we're done, Royce nudges my shoulder. "Hey. I appreciate you doing this, but I don't get why. You're not a student. You won't get any credit."

"Madison told me if we win, she'll give me half her part of the prize."

Royce cuts a look at Madison, expression full of admiration and something else. "I'll go in on that, too. We'll split our parts three ways."

Madison's eyes light up. "Thanks, Royce."

"Meet again tomorrow?"

I hold my breath as Royce and Madison nod.

It's down to Adam.

"Well?" Madison prompts.

I can see his mind turning. I'm not ready for this to slip away.

"Adam's in," I say.

"How do you figure?" he demands.

"You sent Madison the video of me on R.U. DOWN to post."

His jaw tightens. "You can't prove that."

"But I can." Madison arches a brow and I fold my arms.

"You think your parents would like to know you're in the habit of sabotaging your ex-girlfriend?"

He doesn't answer.

"Sorry, Adam. You're overruled," Madison says.

"You look the same, but you've changed," he says to me on our way out the door.

I adjust my bag on my shoulder, feeling lighter than I have in weeks. "You're right. I have."

9

OLIVIA

"**W**ow." I stare in the mirror in the bathroom in my former apartment.

"You look hot," Kat says. She unclips the towel from around my shoulders and shakes it out. "Glad you trusted me instead of going to some random stylist in town?"

"Hell yes."

My hair is in a shiny angled bob that brushes my collarbone.

The rest of it's in a pile on the floor, six or eight inches.

It feels like a weight off my shoulders in more ways than one.

This morning I decided I needed a fresh start.

Yesterday in the lab I proved that I can hold my own in hostile territory.

More than that, it felt good to push for what I want, to hear my own voice and have others listen, too.

I'm a whole new Olivia.

Olivia Gives-No-Fucks Barclay.

"I missed you guys," I say. "We need to hang out."

"Tonight," Kat confirms. "Right, Jules?"

Our other roommate dashes for the door. "Our set designer called in sick and we're way behind on painting."

"No prob. We'll bring beer, you tell us where to show."

"Seven PM?"

I grin. "Done. Now if you'll excuse me, I have a mission on campus. Top secret."

I play with the fresh ends of my hair.

"You left this." Kat pulls a lipstick out of the drawer.

It's the one I wore to Fall Ball.

"Perfect." I slick it on and smile at the result.

I'm wearing jeans, black boots, and a cropped hooded sweatshirt with a motorcycle jacket over top.

I look good.

I text Sawyer.

· · ·

Liv: Where are you?

Repentant Asshole: Covering a make-up exam for a colleague at the University Center.

Bad boy Sawyer Redmond doing public service? For the university no less?

I'll believe it when I see it.

I make my way over there and head into the building.

On my way, I stop at the administrative offices and grab a few brochures from Fall Ball and other initiatives I helped organize so I have copies when I go to apply to other schools.

"Current or prospective student?" the woman at the desk asks.

I force a smile. "Neither."

I'm not getting back into Russell, even if I want to.

But being surrounded by the sights and sounds and smells of it reminds me why I loved this place.

The second floor is home to four windowless classrooms, most of which are only used for exams. Today, the hallways have only a few students, and I peer into the first lecture hall.

Full with a class.

The next one has a closed door and a dozen students spread far apart.

At the head of the class is Sawyer, wearing a jacket over a T-shirt, his hair wild, bent over a lectern on his phone.

He looks totally at home. Dressed up and disheveled at once, one part professor and one part rebel.

Heat makes a beeline south, settling into an ache between my thighs. He's so sexy I bite my lip.

On impulse, I pull out my own phone and text him.

Liv: You look hot when you're being a good boy.

His straight gaze cuts toward the door.

I grin as his eyes meet mine.

There's surprise in them, and the fire that's always there when we connect, whether we want it to be or not.

He crosses to the door and opens it a crack. "I'm proctoring an exam, can I help..." he trails off as he takes in my hair and makeup and outfit.

I can feel his physical response in the thickening of the air between us.

"Why? This isn't your class."

"It's a favor. I seem to owe a few of them."

"What for?"

"Don't worry about it."

He's being deliberately secretive. I want to push him but there's a more important reason for my visit.

I tilt my head toward the hall, and with a look back at the students, he steps outside.

We're still half visible, in case any student gets an idea to cheat.

Which means they can see him, too.

"I need a favor," I say under my breath. "Your keycard."

"Unlike my father, I don't hand it out to students."

"Good thing I'm not a student." The slow smile tugs at my lips. "I need to get into the lab."

He arches a brow in amusement. "The one you're not allowed to go to."

"When'd you start being a rule follower?"

The hallway is empty. I step closer and hook a finger in the pocket of his pants.

I'm blocked from the class' vision by Sawyer's body.

He stiffens, his gaze dropping to my painted lips. His amusement is fading.

That's okay. I'm entertained enough for the both of us.

"Do you like my hair?" I angle my head, giving him a better look.

"It's shorter."

"I think you could still wrap it around your hand." I lick my lips, my fingers sliding into his pocket.

His next exhale is half groan. "Who are you and what have you done with Olivia?"

But his hips move slightly closer to mine.

"There are so many things we could do," I whisper near his jaw. "In the hall. On the stairs. The elevator. Maybe even that water fountain. Hit the button just right, it might feel good."

His hand splays across my collarbone, burning into the bare skin beneath my top.

"I've got lots of ways to make you feel good, sweetheart. I can hit every button that turns you on plus ones you've never imagined."

Heat shimmers down my spine, has my nipples hardening against my bra and a low throb starting between my thighs.

I love Sawyer when he's holding back, but I like him even better when he's not.

"You might be surprised. I have a pretty wild imagination."

"Tell me."

My fingers work in the pocket of his pants. "Okay. There's this one fantasy where you tie me to the bed..."

His eyes darken, his breath getting shallower.

"...and you tease me until I can't stand it. And I'm begging you to let me come, and the only thing you say is... 'Got it.'"

Confusion cuts through his desire. "I've got it?"

"No, *I've* got it." I pull my hand back, holding up his pass. "Thanks."

I turn back to the hallway and start for the stairwell at the end of the hall.

He catches up to me a few steps away. "You're using me."

"Do you regret it?"

He does a quick glance both ways. Then backs me against the wall, his smile fading. "Not for a second."

His lips are so close. It's my turn to suck in a breath.

"You really came here for the keycard?" His voice skims along my skin.

"What else would I have come here for?" I manage.

His mouth crushes mine.

He's hot and wild. As if he's intent on fucking me fully clothed, right here and now.

I can try to be bad. He'll always be better at it.

The first time we did this, I was naïve. Now, I can meet him head-on.

Except when I try to reach for him, he pins my wrists over my head.

My head swims, pleasure and need making me liquid.

I want this version of Sawyer, the one who does favors for colleagues and takes his teaching job seriously.

And I want the version who kisses me until I'm breathless, pushes me to feel and do things I never imagined I would.

"This…" he rasps against my mouth, "…doesn't belong to you."

My heart kicks in my chest, his words ripping me out of the moment.

I pull back to stare in his face.

His eyes are dark, his hair hanging in his face, his mouth bruised from mine.

It takes a moment to notice the keycard in his hand.

Dammit.

He brushes a thumb across my lip, a grin lingering on his swollen mouth. "Now if you'll excuse me, I need to go supervise. Hartman gets an A on this exam, he'll have you to thank. The kid's never done better than a C minus."

With a wink he adjusts my jacket and turns to head back into the classroom.

I'm staring after him, my heart thudding in my chest.

He meant the keycard didn't belong to me.

But he doesn't belong to me either. And this new, responsible version of Sawyer?

I wish he did.

10

SAWYER

"There must be something else you can do." I pace the vice provost's office.

"I won't go over the dean's head," she says from behind her desk.

"But the expulsion is from the university, not the department."

"The evidence furnished by the engineering faculty was compelling, and contravenes our expectations for students. I'm sorry, Professor Redmond. I appreciate you've been campaigning to overturn this for the last month, but nothing has changed."

That's not true.

After what happened yesterday in the hallway, I want Olivia more than ever. But more than that, I want her to get what she deserves.

I'm committed to it.

And after weeks of trying to lobby through the "right" channels, my patience is wearing thin.

"I don't accept that. It's not like she cheated on an exam or committed a felony. Getting expanded keycard permissions is common practice. Not only in our faculty but across departments." Daniel told me students use it to get into practice rooms the university insists on keeping a close handle on even though they're normally empty while the student rooms are packed eighteen hours a day. "In addition, the dean threatened to end her and her classmates' participation in the biggest competition in the country. I still don't know how he got this appointment after what he—"

"That's enough, Professor." Her eyes flash but she recovers quickly. "You were an exemplary graduate of this institution. I understand that you don't feel you need this university anymore, but you will respect it. Particularly given you have a parking spot with your name on it."

She knows how the game is played. She's the second female vice provost of this institution since its inception. It's not easy to wrangle this many departments and keep everyone in line.

"If there's one thing I got from my dad," I start, "it's that Russell is a place for higher learning. It's about merit and possibility. It doesn't matter where you came from, you can make something of yourself here."

I look around the office, the thick burgundy curtains.

"You know the dean treats his staff like shit. The students aren't much better. The only people he has the time of day for are big donors. Maybe that's all you care about too."

"Come on. Come on. Come on..." Olivia croons.

Adam steers the robot through the giant glass tank the team ordered over break, trying to navigate around a post made to be an obstacle in the middle.

It crashes, its fins working uselessly.

"At least it doesn't sink. It used to sink," Royce points out.

"If you want a full assessment of its limitations— probably wise given how quickly finals are approaching—I suggest you find somewhere larger to test it." All four students look toward me.

"Sure. I'll just order a second tank this size. We'll solder them together." Adam stares me down.

"There's a fountain in the middle of campus. How about that?" Olivia suggests, chewing her lip.

I'm still locked in an epic staring contest with the kid in front of me.

"You got a problem?" he growls.

"No. But it seems like you do."

I'm still not happy Olivia's helping the team, both because it could land her in more trouble than she's in, and because I don't trust the others—particularly Adam—not to screw her over.

Despite the new hair and attitude, she can't fool me.

Beneath the smart mouth, she has a kind heart. One that's been wounded by this school and each person in this room.

Me included.

I won't let it happen again.

Though the meeting with the vice provost wasn't great, and despite knowing a lot more about the system, it's frustrating to realize I'm not closer to getting her readmitted.

I've been reluctant to go after the references she wanted to apply to other schools because it feels like admitting defeat. But I'll swallow my pride and start on it, if only to have a contingency plan.

She matters too much to fuck this up.

"We need to find a body of water." Olivia's level voice cuts into my thoughts.

The team looks at one another.

Madison snaps her fingers. "The pool."

"Perfect." Royce rubs a hand over her hair and she ducks away.

"We can bring our own obstacles. That'll give us enough space to let her run," Olivia decides. "Let me call facilities..." she trails off. "I guess one of you guys should."

Madison nods. "I'll do it after lab, or tomorrow before class."

I wait while they go to work on the project, shoulder to shoulder.

"Her?" I prompt to Olivia, who leans over the counter next to me, opposite Madison and Royce. "You called the robot a her."

Olivia cocks her head. "Of course it's a her. All ships are female. And cars."

"Because guys worship them, that's why," Royce comments.

"If it's a her, it must have a name," I insist.

"What about Dory? Like the blue fish from *Finding Nemo*?" Olivia goes on at my blank look, "Have you seriously never seen that movie?"

"I was in high school when it came out."

"And you were too cool to watch it," she teases.

"I was absolutely too cool to watch it."

She rolls her eyes, but my attention lingers on

her curved lips, the way her hair swings over her shoulder as she shakes her head.

I'm thinking again of how she crashed my exam, her hair short and eyes fierce, kissing me to try to get my keycard.

I like seeing her take control. But I miss the innocent version of her, the one who's earnest first and sexy because she is, not because she's trying to be.

"Get a room."

Adam's angry remark has me straightening.

"Hallway. Now." I jerk my head and Adam follows.

"Guys…" Olivia starts. We both ignore her.

I yank the door open without looking back to see if he's following.

When it closes after us, I'm in his face. "You don't want her here, you keep that to yourself."

"Because what you want is the only thing that matters?" He doesn't back down an inch.

"I wish she wasn't here either. She shouldn't be some damned assistant, praying to cash in on a slice of this project."

His shoulders cave and he turns away, as if giving up.

"You hate her," I accuse, and he snorts.

"No."

"You love her." Asking makes my gut twist, but if

he's going to keep trying to make her life difficult, I need to know why.

He shoves a hand through his hair. "It's not that simple. It was always her and me. It was easy and constant and...now it's not."

I don't know what that's like. I never expected anyone to be there, not to mention knew what to do when they were.

Except with Olivia, I started to imagine it.

"Some things in life are easy. None of them are constant," I say. "The second you build your life around another person, it'll get pulled out from under you."

He starts down the hall, and I think he's leaving until he turns back to pace this way. "She deserves better than me, and better than you too. But she wants you. That's why she used that money to bribe the dean."

Surprise has my abs clenching. "That's not true. She did it for herself, and the team."

He holds up his fingers to tick them off one by one. "Liv never does anything big for herself. I'm taking over my parents' company, unless I can somehow get drafted through basketball. Madison wants to leverage it into some charity work. Royce needs it," he concedes, "and Liv would go out of her way to help Royce, but this? This is a big favor. There's one person she'd do anything for."

His implication has me shaking my head. "I have a company waiting for me."

"Right. Because your life was so great before you came here. Let me guess: workaholic, rotating girlfriends or hookups, no social life, no kids. Any of this ringing a bell?" He stares at me pointedly. "You needed Stars more than any of us. *Professor.*"

His assessment of my life is bullshit. He knows nothing about me.

But if the part about Olivia being motivated by helping me is true...

My argument that she chose her school over me doesn't hold water.

If anything, helping me cost her school.

She didn't walk away from me.

Not the way I thought.

Before I can respond, a figure appears at the end of the hall.

"My favorite student." The dean strolls toward us, and every muscle in my body tenses.

My gaze flicks to the window in the door, where Madison and Royce are facing me and Olivia's facing away.

I try to motion to Olivia. *Get her out of here.*

He can't see her here. It'll get the entire team in trouble.

"I want to take a look at the project," the dean suggests.

Adam shrugs. "Sure thing."

What the fuck are you doing?

"I'm sure the dean has other commitments."

"On the contrary, this is important."

The dean reaches for the door and I step between him and it. "Dean, I wanted to ask about a policy question."

He frowns. "Not now, Redmond."

"It's a financial one." I appeal to his interests. "I figured out a way we could combine lab delivery to save the university money."

He looks between me and Adam, wondering why I'm raising it in front of a student.

Because this student is trying to harpoon our efforts, for reasons completely fucking inexplicable to me.

"Some other time."

He reaches past me for the handle and I cut a look over my shoulder.

The dean steps inside to find...

Madison and Royce locked in a heated embrace.

Her fingers fist in his hair, his grab her hips—in desire or surprise, I haven't the first clue.

The dean clears his throat and the students spring apart. Madison rubs at her mouth, and Royce shoves his hands in his pockets. "Dean. We weren't expecting you."

"I figured you'd be working on your project."

"We are. But it's not the best time."

The dean's face turns purple. "What kind of a team are you running here, Professor Redmond?"

He doesn't expect an answer and I don't give him one before he turns and starts back down the hall, muttering to himself.

Once he's gone, I grab Adam's collar and shove him up against the door.

Madison and Royce run over, and Olivia straightens from behind the lab bench where she was hiding.

"Are you trying to get us in even more trouble?"

"No! He's got his sights set on my parents as his next donors. He'll do what I say."

"He'll do what he wants," I correct, releasing the kid.

Madison steps between me and Adam and hits him in the shoulder. "This is our future, asshole. All of us. You can't be playing with it."

My gaze tugs back to Olivia, Adam's words echoing in my head.

Let me guess: workaholic, rotating girlfriends or

hookups, no social life, no kids. You needed Stars more than any of us.

There's one person she'd do anything for.

"You okay?" she asks, crossing to me, her dark eyes full of concern.

I clear my throat and force a smile. "Fine. Let's get back to work."

11
____

OLIVIA

"Does that look like a sex worker to you?" Kat asks, biting her paintbrush between her teeth.

"Um. Is it supposed to?" I cock my head at the pink and black blob painted on the huge sheet of plywood in front of us.

"Hey, Jules. Come over here." Our roommate rounds the set piece she's painting to the one we're working on. "This is clearly a skirt, right? And thigh-high boots?"

"Why are you painting a person? I said an urban wall with a door."

"A *door*," Kat echoes.

"Yeah, a *door*, not a—"

"OH! On it."

I swallow the laugh as Kat goes to work covering up her first attempt.

"You guys didn't need to let me co-opt Hoes Over Brews," Jules says.

"Not co-opting. Collaborating." I step back to inspect my handiwork.

"Art is an important form of expression," Kat agrees, reaching for her beer.

We're backstage in the theater hall surrounded by set pieces and tarps. Helping Jules with her work in progress feels good, not only because I love to assist a friend in need but because painting is strangely cathartic.

"How's living at the dance studio?" Jules asks.

"It's kind of growing on me. I don't use the kitchen much, but the desk is great. I can work on ideas for our project during the day and read, then teach in the afternoons. And when there aren't classes, I dance in the studio."

Using my body that way, without agenda, has been fantastic. I never expected to get back into dance after giving it up, but it's helped me feel grounded and happy in a way I haven't in a long time.

"What about Stars?"

I fill them in on the progress and drama. "Despite

everything, it's starting to feel like we actually have a shot at this."

"If no one catches you and the team wins," Jules says.

"Exactly."

"It's good to have a project," Kat agrees. "I've been busy in the kitchen. Which reminds me, I made you a present." She drops her paintbrush and reaches for her backpack, pulling out a shoebox.

I open it, parting the tissue paper and giggling when I spot the contents.

"It's…enormous. Thank you."

"You're flying solo, the least you could use is some help."

"Notice the glaze," Jules says, pointing to the purple coating.

"It's a real innovation." Kat nods, earnest. "This way I can customize them."

"It could be a side hustle when you become a sex therapist."

"I like knowing I'm helping people. Emotionally, esthetically, all of it."

I take the huge terra-cotta sculpture—not going to call it a sex toy because my body physically hurts at the idea of putting it anywhere near me down there—and set it on the floor next to my things.

"So now that we have your nights planned out..." she starts as I take a sip of my beer.

I check my phone to find a text from my sister.

Emma: Okay, I'm in. But if it turns into a bloodbath, we're out.

Relief seeps through me.

She's been quiet the past week, but thankfully she's going to our parents' for dinner tomorrow.

Which means I'm going, too.

There's also an email from one of my former professors saying that while I received a solid grade in his course last year, he didn't know me well enough given the fifty-plus student cohort to provide a glowing reference letter.

Except I never asked him for a reference.

There's only one explanation.

Sawyer.

"Everything okay?" Jules asks, brushing blonde hair streaked with blue behind her shoulder.

"Totally."

"If it's family drama," she guesses, "it'll pass. Case in point: when I came out, it took a while to blow over. But eventually it did."

"I thought your parents were supportive."

"They were. My grandparents? Not so much. But after an extra-long look in the doorway at family holidays—checking to see if I'm hiding any lesbians behind me I guess—we get on with things, because there's no other answer."

My lips curve. "Have you brought anyone home with you?"

"Not yet. I told my parents about Tess in first year, but they don't love hearing about it. Especially since we're on and off."

She turns back to the set piece she's painting to resemble a city skyline.

"You can talk about it anytime," I say softly. "You know that."

"Yeah. But sometimes it's nice to talk about other stuff. Especially since I see her for play rehearsals all the time." Jules groans. "Falling for someone you can't have sucks. Especially when they ghost you the second they can't have exactly what they want."

Damn if I don't know what that's like.

Sawyer didn't ghost me, at least not physically. He was calling over break, and if anything, I'm the one who didn't want to talk.

But he closed down before that, when I told him I wouldn't go to New York with him. He shuttered his emotions and lashed out, and I can't blame him for being wired that way, but it's hard to love someone whose first instinct is to lock up their heart against any threat, real or perceived.

People change. I've changed.

In lab the other day, his expression was furious when he cornered Adam after the dean showed up.

But it wasn't only anger.

It was fear.

Not for himself, but for me.

He thinks I'm doing a stupid thing by helping with Stars, but he's still willing to protect me.

Now, the email about the reference won't leave my head.

Sawyer's doing what I asked, without trying to get credit for it.

Once, he would have used that as leverage.

Which means what?

It's hard enough to stay strong against his will, his pursuit.

It's near impossible when even my heart wants to give him another chance.

"It's...delicious," Adam's mother says at the dinner table at my parents' new apartment.

I bite into my chicken, chewing twice as much as usual before swallowing.

"I'm so glad." Mom takes a forkful of her own, her face falling. "It's a new oven. We're still getting used to it."

Dinner is Mom, Dad, Adam, and his parents. Mom insisted on trying to make the best of the situation. I braved it because I hoped I'd get to see my sister for the first time since she moved out, but so far, there's been no sign of her.

"I'll refresh drinks," my mom offers.

"Please, let me help." Adam's mother rises from her seat, her chair knocking into the sideboard behind it.

"Couldn't we have found more space?" my dad says under his breath.

"Where, the parking garage?" Mom calls over her shoulder as she heads toward the kitchen, Adam's mom in tow.

Adam cuts a look of pity at me over his glass.

"Adam, how's school?" my dad asks.

"It's busy. The basketball team lost a few games early, and Coach is riding us. I might still be a few weeks from practice"—he glances down at his arm, which is out of the sling but still cradled in his lap—"but the rehab he's got me on is no joke. Plus classes got harder third year, and the competition is taking a lot more time."

"I keep telling him basketball is going to pull him away from his schooling"—his dad shakes his head—"but so far, he refuses to give it up."

"You manage everything so well," Dad says. "I wish my family had your resilience."

"Liv does."

My head snaps up at the sound of Adam's voice.

"She's the most resilient person I know."

Surprise fills me.

In past week, he's kept his opposition to me being on the team to himself.

Either he feels bad for what he said, or he's realized we have a ton of work to do before finals and need all the help we can get.

"Well, if she didn't get herself into so much trouble, she wouldn't have to be." My father smiles.

Adam plants his fork into his chicken breast, releasing the handle so the utensil sticks straight out of the dry meat.

"Sounds like she comes by it honestly."

"Adam!" his mother gasps as she returns to the room, my mother looking startled holding her bottle of wine.

The front door opens and I crane my neck to see Emma and her new fiancé.

He's wrapped in a leather jacket, and she's in a parka from Bergdorf's.

"I thought you weren't coming," Mom says as Emma tugs off her boots.

"Sorry. We got caught in traffic. We don't need to eat," Emma says as they perch on chairs. "Everyone, this is Trey."

"Hey." He scans the table, the eyes I saw warm in the proposal pic now cool and appraising. As if maybe he has some idea what he's walking into.

It's brave of him to come after all that's happened. I suppose he was going to have to show his face eventually, but I'm still impressed.

My mom brings new glasses and sets them in front of Emma and Trey. "Wine?"

"Please," says Emma.

"Um. Sure." Trey nods to my mom.

Dad fists both hands on the table on either side of his plate. "You won't be driving my daughter around after you've been drinking."

"I was trying to be polite."

"What do you do for work?" Adam's father asks. Probably trying to settle the evening down after Adam's outburst.

"My brothers and I own a garage."

There's silence until I break it. "Working on cars

would be cool. I'm in—was in—engineering at school. Just taking a little break."

"Cool."

"Hey, Ems, can I talk to you for a sec?"

She rises and we head for the door.

I shoot Adam a look that I hope communicates, "Don't let them kill Trey."

He nods, almost imperceptible.

Emma and I duck outside into the hallway. Kismet scratches plaintively on the door and we let her out with us.

"How's engaged life?" I start. "Have you picked out napkins for the wedding? If you hire a metal band to play, you'll deny mom her lifelong aim of seeing you use those ballroom lessons she made us both take."

My sister's glare is softened by the twitching of her lips. "The first few days were great. But the second week wasn't what I expected." Emma kneels on the carpet, scratching a grateful Kismet behind both ears. "His brothers who live with us don't like me. But Trey says they've always lived together, and it's not going to change. We live a long way from school, and people are up all night. I fell asleep in class."

"You thought it would be easy?"

"Yes!"

My head falls back. "Emma, I could've told you if you'd talked to me."

When I look back down, Emma's got both arms wrapped around the dog like it's a security blanket. "You're like Mom. You would've told me no. Which is hypocrisy given what you've been doing."

"I wouldn't have told you no! Okay, maybe I would suggested waiting a year. Or three," I concede at her raised brows. "But I'll always be here for you. And it's not hypocrisy."

"You sleeping with your professor? Yeah that's nothing like me dating a guy five years older."

"It is different," I insist. "Sawyer's responsible and serious and—"

"And he never asked you to marry him."

"He asked me to move in with him." My throat dries. "He wanted me to leave school and my friends and follow him. I said no."

Emma straightens, brushing her hands on her legs. "Because you didn't love him."

"Of course I love him."

Love is a simple word for a wholesome feeling.

The way I felt about Sawyer was thrilling and terrifying, consuming and destructive. He peeled back the layers of my life and shone a light on them, showing me how deficient they were not because I wasn't trying hard enough, but because I was trying too hard to do the wrong things.

"Then why not?"

"Because I was afraid I'd be betraying myself by going with him."

"Sounds like you betrayed yourself by turning him down." Emma wraps her skinny-strong arms around me. "I love you, okay? But don't put that on me."

12

SAWYER

"You wanna get me out of this?" I ask Captain Jack.

He swims the length of his tank, impassive and unmoved.

"You're less help than Dad was," I grumble.

I finish feeding the fish and grab my coat, heading for the car.

If there was a way I could escape going to the dean's winter social, I would. But it's hosted every year, with a special speaker, and I need to get support for Olivia's references since I came up empty on my initial attempt.

This is one thing I can do to help secure a bright future for her.

Not the one she expected, but one every bit as good.

I've parked in a campus lot and am halfway up the walk to the dean's house when a shape tumbles out of the bushes into me.

"Professor Redmond!" the female voice exclaims.

"Madison?!"

She straightens, brushing snow and evergreen needles off her coat.

"I trust there's a reason you're hiding in the hedge outside the dean's residence."

Her expression is sheepish. "I need to get into the social. The special guest runs Engineers without Borders."

"The event is for faculty."

She sucks in a breath. "And their plus-ones."

Surely she can't be this dense. There's no way I can walk into that building with a twenty-year-old on my arm and walk out again alive.

"You realize me bringing a student to this is professional suicide."

"I know but...can you just get me in at the door then ditch me? Please, Professor. I've been trying to talk to this man for months. It means everything to me. Haven't you ever wanted anything this badly?"

It's bad for my already scarred reputation, which I need pieces of to help Olivia.

But Madison is looking up at me like I can grant her dying wish.

There were times in my life when people in power had the chance to help.

More often than not, they didn't. Even when it cost them nothing to say yes.

Helping my student now could hurt me and those I care about...

So why is it so hard to say no?

"Fine." Her eyes widen in delight. "But the moment we're inside, you're gone. No one sees us together."

"I'm allergic to you," she vows, stepping toward my side.

"Allergic might be overkill," I mutter as we start toward the walkway.

"I mean it. You're abhorrent. I won't even look at you."

"Thank you."

She falls into step with me. At the doorway, a male attendant in a suit and bow tie is checking names.

"Professor Redmond," I say. "And this is my...guest."

There are already eyes glancing over.

"You won't regret this." She grins and dashes off into the throng.

I shake my head. I already do.

The house is grand, with a double staircase

leading upstairs. There's a poster board on an easel featuring the man Madison wanted to get in to see.

Faculty mill about, sipping cocktails.

The dean is nowhere in sight, so I begin my campaign to get Olivia references.

Thirty minutes later, I've gotten three no's, one yes, and one maybe.

The sound of the dean's laughter drifts into my ears.

"You must get exposure from events like these," he's saying to a man whose face is familiar—he's the guy speaking, I realize. "All I'm pointing out is that a speaker fee is surely extraneous."

"We're a non-profit. The speaker fee goes to help support our programming."

He excuses himself as another faculty member cuts in.

I look around to see where Madison is, hoping she got her chance.

She catches sight of him the same time I spot her, standing on the other side of the room, an untouched glass of wine clutched in both hands.

Her lips move as if she's giving herself a pep talk. Then with a tiny nod, she starts to cross to the man.

I begin to turn away when her progress is impeded.

The dean slides in front of her. "Madison. You're the last person I expected to see here."

"Dean. I was hoping to speak to your guest. I'm a huge fan."

"This isn't a student event."

"I understand. A faculty member admitted me."

"Who?"

"Um. New prof. Girl, actually. Female prof." He stiffens, as if to argue when Madison flashes a big smile and tilts her head. His gaze glides over her simple black dress and heels, lingering too long on places it shouldn't.

"I might be able to arrange a meeting. But first, I'm being a terrible host. Let me show you the house."

He glances toward the top of the stairs, and my stomach curls.

"It's okay, Dean. I couldn't take you away from all these people—"

"Nonsense. What's a house like this for if not to show off?"

I leap into action.

"It's really quite ordinary." Madison looks up at me as I approach, relief crossing her features. "Let's go find your speaker. It's a school night and I'm sure you need to be getting home."

I place a hand lightly on her back, feeling her shaking.

"You okay?" I murmur once we're clear of the dean.

She nods tightly and I drop my hand.

"You want this?" I gently take the glass she's clutching tight enough to break.

"No. I don't even like wine."

I set it on a nearby table and return to help her find the speaker.

He's in the next room, surrounded by three faculty.

Her relief is replaced with disappointment as she sees the number of people wanting to speak with him. "You don't need to wait," she says, "this could take a while."

"Nonsense. There might be polite rules of society, but I never learned them." I grin and after a moment, her mouth tips up too. "Let's go."

We're nearly at the grouping when she grabs my arm, pulling me back. "Thank you. For back there…"

It's my turn to be surprised. "You don't have to say that."

"Yeah, I do. Because most people would rather look the other way. It's easier to pretend it never happened so they don't have to say anything."

I introduce myself and Madison to the speaker, but I'm on autopilot.

Most people would rather look the other way.

The dean is going to pay for being a piece of shit.

Am I so different?

The thought creeps up from somewhere so deep and dark I never realized it was there.

As I keep an eye on Madison, talking animatedly to the speaker, I turn over my own situation.

I pursued Olivia. I was the powerful one.

Yes, she wanted me before she knew I was her professor. But once she knew, I pressed on it.

I used our attraction as an excuse.

It's not one.

Neither is the fact that I fell for her.

I was reckless with her heart and her future.

The twin urges to self-destruct and to atone wrench at me until it feels as if I'm being ripped in two.

I could go home and drown myself in alcohol until I don't feel a damn thing.

Instead, I get in my car and drive.

13

OLIVIA

It's cold.

The rain has turned to snow, leaving the hills glistening and frosted.

I'm sitting in the middle of the studio in my dance clothes. I didn't stay overnight in New York, instead grabbing a train back from the city.

My final exchange with Emma echoed in my head the entire way.

"Sounds like you betrayed yourself by saying no."

Maybe she's right.

Sawyer and I have made each other's lives harder. But we've made each other better. I'm stronger. He's more compassionate.

Most of all, my world is brighter and more full of possibility with him in it.

The crunch of snow and gravel under tires has me running to the window.

What the…

The Mercedes is familiar even through the snow.

I'm at the front door in a second, unlocking it.

The cold air scorches my lungs, but it doesn't matter when Sawyer cuts the engine and shifts out.

He slams the door and crosses to me in a few short strides. His wool coat hits at his knees, and with the long hair and handsome features, he could be some fairy-tale prince. But from the tension on his face, he looks more like the tormented beast.

"Do you know what time it is?" I ask.

"Late." Whatever's on his mind shifts to take a back seat as he searches my expression. "What's wrong?"

"Nothing. I went for dinner back home, and had a talk with Emma…"

A creak at my back has me turning to glance up the stairs.

"You should probably go."

He wedges a foot in the door. "There's something I need to say first."

Whatever's on Sawyer's mind, I'm not sure I want to hear it. But I'll listen.

I owe him that much.

Suddenly the torment is back, his jaw working. "I need a second."

I turn and head back into the studio, the front door clicking softly the only indication he's following me.

When I reach the studio, he's still silent.

It's too quiet. So I put on music and return to what I was doing.

I work back into it, one movement at a time. Bending and leaping and turning, my body heats up again.

Air in, air out.

Sawyer fills the doorway like a shadow.

"I saw myself tonight."

I finish a sequence and come to a stop in front of the mirror, panting as I meet his gaze in the mirror. "What do you mean?"

"I saw a version of who I could have been." He comes closer. "You were right to call us a mistake. I never should have pursued you."

I relevé on one foot, bending my knee to my side and lifting my arms above my head. "It wasn't a mistake."

When I start to turn, he catches me, steadies me. "It was worse than that. A mistake implies a lack of culpability. It's all my fault. Your expulsion. The position we're in now. I didn't mean for it to happen, but I'm responsible for this."

"Then you're also responsible for trying to get me back into school."

"Which hasn't worked," he grinds out.

I ignore him. "And for trying to arrange for professors to give me references."

He grabs my knee and spins me to face him. My hands grab his shoulders for balance.

"No matter what's happened with us," I continue, "I know that you want the best for me."

He goes still. "I don't. I do," he amends at my startled look, "but that's not the only reason I do these things for you."

"Then what is?"

The music streams from the stereo, a lullaby that builds the cocoon around us. In this studio as familiar as any, it's Sawyer that smells like home.

"I'm in love with you," he whispers. "And it's fucking killing me, Olivia. I don't know myself anymore. I'm not the man I was, and I'm not the man I want to be for you, but I'm trying. And every time I fall down, every time I disappoint you, it reminds me I don't deserve you. Maybe I never will."

My chest expands, heart thudding impossibly against my ribs.

Sawyer loves me?!

"I fucked this up at every turn," he goes on, his fingers flexing on my thigh. "From the moment I saw you, all I knew was that I wanted to be close to you. That the world was better now that I knew you existed. And coming back to this place, I was hurting and angry and I had no intention of sticking around. When I found out you were a student, I told myself to stay away. But I couldn't."

Sawyer loves me...

His inhale is ragged. "When you turned me down about New York, it felt like you were saying no to me. To us. Choosing your life over me, like everyone else has. But you were right to do it."

Sawyer.

Loves.

Me.

I brush my thumbs down his jaw and his teeth snap shut.

"I was scared," I whisper. "Not right. Yes, you pursued me. And maybe it was wrong. But I wanted you, too. I might have grown up with money and opportunities, but my world was small before I met you. You made me feel alive and free and desired. You made me believe in things I never believed before."

His mouth crushes mine.

He's warm and fierce and raw.

Except entwined with his dominance, it's searching, as if he needs an answer he can only find in my lips, my arms.

He pulls me hard against him, and every cell of my body sings out.

I kiss him hard, my hands fisting in his hair. The strands are damp from the snow. His mouth is warm and I want all the contrasts he has to offer. Warm and cold, brash and thoughtful, cruel and kind.

"I need you," he grunts.

I open my mouth to agree, then reality catches up to me. I don't want to piss Theresa off, but sending Sawyer away right now, spending another moment not touching him, might kill me.

I could bring him up the stairs, but if Theresa catches us, we're done for.

I grab his hand and some boots by the door and stomp outside.

He looks up at the fire escape with a resolved sigh.

"You climbed a tree to get into my room the first night," I remind him with a grin.

"Oh, I remember. I still have bruises." His voice makes the hairs on my arms lift. "Catch you up there."

Five minutes later, I've lowered it down and he's climbed up.

The moon shines on his hair, and snowflakes stick to his sweater.

He leans in the window and I meet him, breathless.

My entire body shivers and it's not from the cold. My nipples are hard through my leotard, and he's barely inside when he drags me against him and reaches down to cup my ass.

"We have to be quiet," I plead.

"I can handle that. Can you?"

He walks me across the room, feet creaking on the floor. He sets me on the edge of the bed, leaning me back. Then strips his sweater over his head, dragging his shirt along with it.

In the full moon from the window, his body is silhouetted in the darkness.

He's raw and real, a god made human. Glorious and impatient and adoring.

He peels my leotard off my shoulders, brushing the skin it reveals with his lips. My tights get dragged along for the ride.

He shifts over to turn on the bedside lamp with the shell I bought.

"Cute."

"Thanks. I picked it out." I'm equal parts pleased he likes it and desperately distracted by my near nudity and his evident desire.

"Then we both have good taste." I'm in only my panties as he rocks back to look at me. "I picked you out."

My lips curve, my heart beating faster as he takes every inch of me in.

From the low groan, he likes what he sees.

"Missed this view, sweetheart. You looking up at me like this…"

I reach for his chest, needing the heat of his skin under my greedy hands.

He hisses out a breath as my fingertips skim his flat nipples, running south over the hard muscles of his chest and abs.

"You afraid I'm going to break you? Or that I'm going to make you wait for the privilege?"

I can't answer because Sawyer's hot mouth descends to my breasts, and I grab his shoulders to keep grounded. His tongue and teeth torment me as if he's re-learning the shape of me, testing how hard he can bite and tease before I pass out.

When his hands slide between my thighs, teasing the inside of my legs, I bite my tongue to keep from moaning.

His mouth returns to the undersides of my breasts, licking and sucking every inch of me like I taste different everywhere and he wants to leave no part unsampled.

I'm in love with you.

It recasts everything between us. Each kiss isn't just hungry, it's worshipful. Every touch isn't only greedy, it's grateful.

Eventually, when I'm panting and writhing, he starts down my stomach.

"Do I get to touch you?" I protest.

"When I'm done touching you."

"When will that be?"

He pauses to raise his head before reaching the tops of my thighs, eyes sparking with humor and happiness. "Don't hold your breath."

I bite my lip. Dammit, I want to argue with him. But I love how he looks at me right now.

Except every assessment flies from my head as his mouth lowers to the place where I'm already wet and aching.

His tongue licks a long stroke that flicks my clit at the end, and my hips snap up to meet him like a puppet on a string.

"That's it, sweetheart. Give me all of it," he rumbles against my skin.

I try to hold out some sense of composure, but when his fingers join the party, there's no way I can play it cool.

I grab a pillow and press it to my face. I want to

watch him go down on me, but it's this or wake up Theresa and the bird, guaranteed.

He murmurs his approval against my wetness, his talented mouth and fingers going to work in a way that reminds me no amount of solo sessions can compare to him.

"Sweet fucking girl."

His tongue has me dancing under him, and I can't resist tempting fate by pushing the pillow aside so I can watch his dark head move between my thighs.

But when he presses two fingers into me, pushing past my body's resistance and sinking inside, my knuckles whiten on the pillow.

His chuckle is hungry. "That's my Cherry. Always ready for me."

Pleasure weaves knots deep inside me, braiding together into layers of delight until I'm so tight I'm ready to explode.

"Come on me." His words vibrate against my clit. "Let me taste you."

My body tightens, the climax impossible to stop even if I wanted to. The coiled need deep inside me melts into ecstasy, rippling outward from my core.

I twist under him as he holds me down. His tongue licks at me, offering no relief from the sensations.

"Stop," I gasp, shoving the pillow at his head to try to get him to relent. "Sawyer, please."

He only changes the rhythm of his torment, light licks and slow strokes against my walls that wake the parts of me I thought had tapped out after the first orgasm.

He's going to kill me.

Soon I'm coming again, delirious from the feelings. My body shakes and trembles as the aftershocks rock through me.

Sawyer shifts onto the bed, stripping out of his jeans and boxer briefs. I'm boneless when he scoops me up and settles me in his lap facing him.

We're not done.

Sawyer threads both hands in my hair, pressing my forehead to his. His lips brush mine. He tastes like me, and I love it.

His cock is thick and so hard he's leaking. I reach down to brush a finger across the head of him, sticky and swollen.

"I've dreamed about being inside you. Nothing between us," he whispers, and my heart accelerates against my ribs. "I'm not asking, because I have no right, but..."

I rub my lips across his, cutting off his words. "I'm on the pill. And I haven't been with anyone."

His eyes darken, nostrils flaring. "I haven't either. In months. Even before you."

I want this, too. So much.

I wrap my hand around his cock.

He's sticky, and I'm spreading it everywhere. He lets me play a minute, squeezing his thick shaft as I enjoy his reaction.

Then his hands are on my hips, lifting me and setting me on his cock.

I inhale in shock as my body stretches to let him in. Once he's halfway inside I adjust my legs on either side of his hips before shifting back down on him.

"Every inch, sweetheart," he groans. "I'm yours."

It's thrilling, and I arch back to take him deeper.

"I missed you," I whisper.

"I've only ever been here," he responds. "I'm only ever with you."

Sawyer leans in, pressing his lips to my throat. His words and body make me throb.

Yes. This is what I want. What I need.

It might have felt like a mistake, but it was a revelation.

I start to move but he stops me, grabbing my ass and lifting and lowering me on him.

He's doing all the work, but I'm being worshipped.

The tension builds low in my stomach, and coupled with the sweet burn where we're joined, I know I won't last.

His thrusts deepen as he changes the angle, hitting the front of my channel.

My body clenches around him, and I swear he thickens more inside me.

His strokes get rough, shallow, and my breath hitches. I lean back, my palms dropping to the soft, quilted bedspread.

Sawyer's gaze drags to my breasts, bouncing against my ribs with every thrust.

More.

More.

More.

His nostrils flare, flames dancing behind his eyes.

His groan echoes off the wall and I clap a hand over his mouth to quiet him. Dark eyes fill with need and appreciation, and when I pull back, he's smiling.

"Come here."

He tugs me down over him so my breasts brush his chest, but his rhythm doesn't slow. The change in the feeling has me gasping, and his pant against my ear feels as if he's run a marathon.

"That's my girl. Mine. Now. Always."

Sawyer says it over and over, until I don't even know if he realizes he's saying it. But the words are a backdrop to the building eruption within me, and soon I can't come back from the edge he's dragging me over.

His grip on me tightens, hips pistoning roughly between my thighs as every muscle in him contracts.

I feel him explode inside me, feel my body milking him for what feels like minutes until my damp forehead falls against his shoulder.

Brushing a kiss across my temple, he lifts me off him then pulls down the covers to reveal the sheets beneath. He tucks us between them, the weave feeling refreshingly cool on my hot skin.

Sawyer pulls my hips against his, facing each other and lying on our sides.

He grins, brushing the hair from my face with careful fingers. "Tell me about this dinner you went to."

"You really want to know?" I grimace, starting to flop back on the pillow. He drags me back so I can't avoid his gaze.

"I never had family dinners. Humor me."

I sigh. "It was the first time everyone met Trey together. Emma's surprised everything isn't easier." I wrinkle my nose, something coming back to me for the first time.

"It never stops being hard." He presses a kiss to

my palm that leaves me tingling long after his lips are gone. "But I meant what I said. You're mine."

When he strokes a hand down my side, my entire body shivers.

"Maybe it'll take you time to realize it. Though from our current position," he goes on as I arch a brow, "I think you're coming around."

Being here in Sawyer's arms is everything. But it's one thing to know he loves me, and another to throw myself completely over the cliff. Being with him reminds me how easy it is to get swept out to sea.

Everything in my life is precarious right now. I can't take that chance.

"I guess it's good I'm not a Russell student," I say. Even if I wasn't in Sawyer's class, that would complicate an already complicated situation.

He strokes a hand down my bare shoulder. "I haven't given up on getting you back in, you know. And I won't."

The hairs on my neck lift. "But you've been getting me references for other schools."

"It's called a contingency plan. You'll finish your degree at a good school because you've worked for it, but you deserve *this* degree. *This* school."

I start to sit up. "Sawyer—"

"No. You've been working as hard as any student. Harder, in fact. And I will do whatever it takes to get you re-enrolled so you can have everything you deserve."

God, he's stubborn.

"And if I disagree?"

He traces the curve of my breast with a lazy finger. "Then I'll have to convince you I'm right."

His mouth bends toward mine, his hair tickling my cheek as his claims my lips with his.

The way Sawyer kisses makes me feel like my mind is separating from my body, floating off into a state of total bliss.

Until he hardens against my stomach, and the throb between my legs reminds me how empty I feel without him there.

"Mmm. Since we're talking about school…" Before I can lose my head, I pull back an inch. "The pool we tested Dory in is nowhere close enough to a real environment to give us the data to present in California."

He frowns. "Maybe I can help with that."

"How?"

"Leave it to me."

I'm curious, but more than that, I love that he's taking this off my list.

"Perfect," I hum. "I've more than pulled my weight for the first part of the semester, so I'm sure you and the others can figure it out from here," I tease, trailing a hand down his chest to the trail of hair gracing his hard stomach.

His tight exhale is half laugh, half groan. "I said I'd do this one thing, but don't think you can slack off going forward, Miss Barclay. There will be zero special treatment."

"Really?" I blink at him. "But what if someone literally fucked my brains out?"

Sawyer rolls overtop, pressing me down into the mattress.

"Then I'll have to fuck them right back in."

14

<hr>

<h1 style="text-align:center">SAWYER</h1>

hen I get to the Midtown offices of the company I co-founded, I take the elevators up to our floor.

The receptionist lifts her brows when she sees me.

"I'm here to see Graham," I say.

"Is he expecting you?"

"That would take all the fun out of me surprising him."

Without waiting for her to challenge me, I head through the departments to one of the twin corner offices.

It's austere, corporate. Not like my office on campus where you can practically smell the history, hear the bustle of students outside talking about their weekends and music and whatever assignment they have due.

Olivia was correct when she said the pool didn't provide enough challenge or context for Dory. The team needs to know more about how robots would be used in real life.

Which is why I'm back here in a place I vowed never to return to.

My former business partner is on the phone when I walk in, his jacket slung over the back of his chair. When he spots me, he straightens in his seat. "I'm going to have to call you back."

He clicks off, eyes widening. "Sawyer. You're not supposed to be here."

"You wish I wasn't here. There's a difference."

"The settlement—"

"The settlement gave me a bunch of cash, as if that made up for leaving the business I co-founded for a sham."

His mouth snaps shut.

He's having a real Scrooge moment, because I am a ghost from his past. All I'm missing is the clanking chains.

"Why *are* you here?" he demands.

"The environmental department."

I fill him in on my request, and he shakes his

head. "I can't give you company contacts. You're no longer affiliated with..."

He trails off as I sink into the chair opposite his desk, reaching for the little bronze plaque on a wooden block with his name and "CEO" that sits on the blotter.

I turn the nameplate over in my fingers, picking at the corner with a fingernail.

Graham makes a little grunt. I ignore him.

The plaque comes loose, peeling away.

I rip it off and hold it in one hand and the block in the other. "Did you know this was glued on? There are these little nailheads, but I guess they're decorative. Shitty workmanship."

Graham glares at me but picks up his phone and hits a number. "Can you please come into my office? Thanks, Dwayne."

I set both the block and the plaque on his desk and rise, turning to see a guy in a suit enter and look at me the same way Graham did.

"Dwayne. How's the department?"

"You didn't hear? I'm VP now."

Which means Graham is grooming him to take on my responsibilities.

The guy is a piece of crap. He's a handsy drunk and cheats on his wife.

"Congratulations on the promotion."

My tone is flat but he grins, oblivious. "Thanks, man. I appreciate that."

"Sawyer needs an introduction. To one of our engineering clients."

He spreads his hands. "Anything we can do. You're still family, you know that."

The kind of family that doesn't speak to one another.

"They're coming in soon to work on a project today. You want to talk to them now?"

I don't want to do it on this turf, don't want them to know what I'm working on.

"No. I'll follow up directly."

He pulls up his phone and forwards me some contact info. "There you go. Anything else?"

"That's it."

I rise from my chair.

"Good to see you, Sawyer," Graham says.

I don't shake his hand as I turn for the door.

Heading back down the hall, there are more than a few curious faces.

I smile at a few, then I get in the elevator.

But as I hit the button, I realize I'm not alone.

The young woman in the corner is dressed in a suit too mature for her years, her hair tugged back in a tidy ponytail.

She recognizes me the same time I do her.

Only her eyes widen in surprise as my stomach curls inward.

"Hello, Christine."

The doors slide closed, painfully slow, and we begin our descent.

"Well, this is awkward." I cut a look at the camera in the corner. "Fortunately, we're well supervised, so you won't make anything up on your father's behalf."

She presses her back into the corner, wrapping her arms around her. "I didn't."

"Really? It's a bit late for that." I force my hands, fisted at my sides, to loosen. No matter what our history, I never want a woman to feel afraid of me. I'm acutely aware of that now.

The floors click by, one after another.

"Maybe it's for the best." I keep my voice as calm as possible. "If you hadn't done that, I wouldn't have gone to teach at Russell. And I wouldn't have met her."

Curiosity edges into her misery. "Who?"

"The girl who makes my world turn. The one I'd break every rule in the book for."

The doors ding and slide open and I head out without looking back.

My chest relaxes instantly when I'm out into the lobby.

By the time I check my phone to find the

promised introduction in my email, I'm almost content.

Wonder of wonders.

The last time I was here, I was practically dragged out.

Now, I'm a breath away from whistling.

Is this what life is supposed to feel like?

Since last night, I've felt more myself.

The sense of warmth under my ribs that hasn't faded since I woke up in Olivia's bed and snuck out the fire escape the same way I entered, her flushed laughing face over me.

I told her I loved her.

She didn't say it back.

Do I want her to?

Hell, yes. But I'm not going to fuck this up by pressing too hard.

Not yet, anyway.

When I head back out to my car, my strides are bigger, longer.

The city rises up around me.

As a kid, I wanted to get here. Until I started college, when I thought for a moment I could be a professor like Lancaster.

Before Russell made an offer to extend my appointment, I was planning to come back here. I

still have an expensive lease on an apartment in
Midtown.

I could be here right now, working with Tate. But
I'd be another guy in a suit and dress shoes, taking
meetings and making deals and binging espresso
and eating takeout. Instead, I'm living in my father's
house and teaching lectures and trying to figure out
how to get a student project across the finish line.

Maybe Adam was right. There is something to
life at Russell, however fleeting it might be and
however backward the path that returned me there.

I'm halfway to the car when my phone jumps
with a text.

Cherry: How did it go?

Sawyer: Very well.

Cherry: YES. OMG I love you.

My heart stutters in my chest and I pull up.

She means because I did her a solid. It's not reci-
procity for my confession last night.

Even though she's the first woman I've ever said those words to.

I didn't say them for her. I said them for me.

Because they're true, and holding them in was burning a hole inside me.

Still, even if her text is playful, I don't have to take it that way.

Sawyer: I love you too.

When I tuck the phone away, her face flashes in my mind, along with Christine's.

It feels as if I've done a good deed today, and it wasn't as terrible as I anticipated.

I want to do another.

A woman answers when I press the button. "Hello?"

"Mrs. Barclay. Sawyer Redmond. I'd like to speak with you about your daughter."

She buzzes me up.

I head in the glass doors and take the elevator up.

When I get down to the door, I knock.

There's no sound for a long time, then eventually shuffling.

"I'm still adjusting to having to open two doors. With the townhouse, you just opened the door and..." She gestures with an elegant hand.

It's not the first time I've encountered this woman, but now that I have longer to look, I see where Olivia got her beauty and poise. Her mother is graceful, with a slim face and willowy figure and dark hair devoid of gray.

"Which one?" she asks as I follow her inside.

"Which what?"

"Which daughter. Both have had their share of drama recently."

This woman is used to having people strive to impress her. Hell, even I can feel the pressure to do it.

But that's not why I'm here.

I hold up a hand, chest height. "This high. Smart. Engineer. Dancer. Can undercut you with a single comment."

Her brow arches.

"We met once before," I go on, "at the basketball game at Russell."

She nods, recognition setting in. "Of course. I figured you weren't affiliated with the bikers. The hair notwithstanding."

The fuck is wrong with my hair?

"Wine? Beer? Soda?"

I wave her off. "I'm fine, thank you. I'm driving."

She gets a glass of wine for herself and gestures to the dining table.

"I have a twenty-year-old daughter who was kicked out of school and an eighteen-year-old daughter who ran off with a biker last month." She reaches for her wine and drains half the glass at once. "You're the professor who couldn't keep his hands to himself."

The descriptor makes me bristle. But honestly, it's fair.

"I'm sure you've been worried about Olivia. I want you to know she's an incredible woman, and that someone is looking out for her."

Her smile is tight. "You're handsome, Sawyer Redmond. My husband was, too. He was a prestigious money manager, provided everything. I gave him children. He didn't hold up his end of the bargain. Maybe it was fate that I didn't hold up mine, with how the girls are behaving. I was a dancer. I quit with my best years still ahead of me. Do you know what it's like to give up your career, what you have in hand, before you've achieved everything you wanted?"

"Yes."

Her eyes narrow, curious.

"I know exactly how it feels to lose something, to tell yourself you gave it up by choice, but at night when you can't sleep, you ask whether you really gave it up or whether it was taken from you. But if you admit it was taken, it's like admitting you have no control over your life."

She leans in, folding her arms.

"And I don't know anything about your relationship with your husband, but I can tell you that even if I didn't take care of Olivia, she could take care of herself." I debate how much to say without betraying confidence. "Has she told you what she's doing?"

"Only that she's working part-time at a dance studio."

"She's teaching lessons while also running the engineering team. For no credit, because she's a good person."

"And you allow this?"

My chest tightens. "I'm not sure I could stop her if I wanted to. But yes, I want her to get a degree, because she's worked her ass off. She's planning to apply to another school."

She turns the glass in her hands, studying the rim. "For the longest time, I couldn't understand why she wanted that. I hoped she'd find a man who could take care of the more...pedestrian necessities of life. It's only recently I've come to appreciate her desire." I resist the urge to look around the apartment, her words sinking in. She looks up before I can, sharp eyes meeting mine. "Why can't she get back into Russell?"

"There's red tape for days."

Her lips curve, like Olivia's but minus the sweetness. "Do you know what that means? Somewhere, a man made a decision, and covered it up with words so he's immune to the consequences."

I turn that over. "Perhaps, but—"

"It wasn't a committee that decided my daughter wouldn't be in school. It was a man." She starts down the narrow hallway from the living room, motioning me to follow.

We pass through a doorway into the bedroom. I'm a beat away from turning and leaving when she crosses to the closet.

"Hold this." She passes me a box, then stands on her toes to reach for a shoebox.

She takes it to the bed, setting it down and lifting the lid.

On top, there are photos.

"That's you?" I ask.

"This one. This one is Olivia." Her lips curve.

I take the photos from her. Both are on stage in a performance, both in tutus with slicked-back hair.

"You look the same."

"It's the uniform."

"I meant because you both look happy."

"Don't get any ideas. I'm still a married woman. Though in a few months I might not be."

She lifts a stack of photos, then another, out.

Beneath is an envelope.

"If there's one thing I understand, it's men. You find the man who made the decision, and motivate him properly, and you'll get her back into that school."

She presses the envelope into my hand. Inside is what feels like a stack of bills.

"I can't take this."

"If you truly care about her, you will. If you can get her back into that school, I want to help keep her there."

15

OLIVIA

"Allie, take off the coat."

The dance mom holds out a hand at the child as my group of guppies and I wait at the bottom of the steps leading to the outdoor stage.

"I don't want to."

"I made you this leotard especially for today."

I hold up a hand at the overeager dance mom. "And it's fifty degrees out."

"She'll learn to be tough."

No, she'll learn to hate dance.

I motion to the woman, and she leans in. "One of my dance teachers in New York always said that frostbitten fingers can ruin the most elegant lines."

I keep a straight face as I say it. The mom blinks at me but backs off.

"Nicely done." Daniel appears at my shoulder,

grinning. "Must be a tough job wrangling a dozen kids."

"It's harder wrangling the parents. It's as if their ego will live or die on the performance of their child."

I survey the six- and seven-year-olds milling about as we wait our turn.

"Andy's been excited about this for the last week. It's been a rough time for him lately, between school and...other things. But he's been practicing every afternoon."

My chest squeezes. "That's awesome, Daniel. It shows. And it's actually a good gig; they're awfully cute."

"You're awfully cute."

The voice from behind me has the hairs lifting on my bare arms under my coat.

I spin to see Sawyer, in a wool coat and scarf and jeans, his hair blowing in the winter wind. He looks delicious, and I soak in the sight of him under the bright sun, made brighter against the snow.

"You got something under that?" He nods to my puffer jacket.

"Maybe you'll find out, Professor Redmond."

"Okay, I'll be over in the audience watching. The kids, not whatever this is," Daniel says, gesturing to us before turning away.

Sawyer steps closer. I'm intimately aware of the crowd surrounding us, and the inches between his chest and mine.

"I brought you something from New York." He reaches into his pocket and produces a sheet of paper, pressing it into my gloved hand. "Environmental non-profit contact to weigh in on Dory. It's in your email, but I swiped this brochure too."

Excitement flows through me. "Just what I always wanted." I wiggle my brows at him. "Thank you. I'll follow up with them."

"Mm-hmm. You seemed more excited yesterday when you texted."

His stare warms on me, expectant and teasing at once.

Suddenly all I can think of is what I wrote to him.

I love you.

A flush crawls up my face.

I didn't mean it like that.

Except I totally meant it like that.

But I'm not telling him I love him on text.

Or in the middle of a crowd in public, for that matter.

The announcer calls for us.

"I have to go." I brush my lips over Sawyer's once, too fleeting, catching a flicker of disappointment he hides behind his smirk before I round up my kids and shepherd them on stage.

It's a football game, and we're part of the pre-game entertainment. I taught them a penguin dance and found them all knit hats with penguin faces.

I found one for me, too.

From the crowd, Theresa grins and films it on her phone.

Some drunk frat guys start imitating the penguin dance, and I swallow my laughter.

My roommates are out there, too, and I nod to them as I lead my train of penguins around the stage.

Deafening applause and drunken shouting greet us when we finish.

I get the kids back down and handed off to their parents one at a time.

"That was fabulous!" Betty, from the engineering department, descends, wearing her football jersey. "It's good to see you here. I had no idea you were back."

"Yeah, I'm teaching dance. Of course I'd love to be back in school, but it's not likely."

Her expression darkens. "If it was up to me, honey, neither you nor Sawyer would've been punished for what happened. The dean was out of line. Not for the first time, either. But"—her smile returns—"that's not worth thinking about today."

She disappears and I start to search the crowd for Sawyer.

Before I can, there's a text on my phone.

Mom: I enjoyed meeting your professor.

What?

No.

No, no, no.

My head snaps up as my roommates descend.

"Hey, penguin girl!" Kat shouts.

"That was crazy cute," Jules agrees. "What's wrong?"

I lower the phone, numb, and find Sawyer's gaze through the crowd.

He pushes his way through to me.

"Ladies," he says. "I'm going to borrow this one—"

"Did you talk to my mom?!"

Kat's eyes go round and Jules gasps.

Sawyer doesn't flinch. "Yes."

"When were you going to tell me?"

"Sometime after you finished your performance."

Sawyer went to my house. No, the new apartment. He stepped into my space, talked with the people I've fought my whole life against.

"Why?"

Now he looks past me, up into the stands. "Because I wanted to let her know that you're all right."

"So you told her what I'm doing here? You sat down and had a full conversation about me, without me." He starts to pull me toward him, but I glance past him to Daniel and Andy, and some other guys who seem to be with them. "I'll catch up with you later."

"Tonight."

"Or tomorrow."

His gaze narrows and he steps toward me, tugging off his mittens. One hand slips in my jacket, the other under my shirt so his rough palm caresses my back.

"Don't try to push me away." His lips caress the shell of my ear. "I'm an expert, I can recognize it for miles. And I won't let you."

With a look that's warning and tender at once, he turns and heads toward Daniel and the others.

"Thank you for agreeing to speak with me," I say on the video call.

"Our pleasure," the woman answers. "When Dwayne says we should meet, I'm happy to accommodate."

I'm still upset with Sawyer about seeing my mom, but I need to keep this project moving. Fortunately, his contact was quick to schedule the conversation.

At her side is a young woman about my age dressed in a tailored blouse, her hair pulled back in a low ponytail.

"We're building a robot to help with environmental remediation in the oceans," I start, "and I was hoping you could tell me more about how you interface with industrial partners. If this robot does what we want, how could we work research labs and nonprofits to help ensure it gets used?"

"Well, most of our projects start out from an identified need in the ecosystem. Funders at the national, state, or sometimes municipal level provide funding to study and remediate these issues."

She talks me through a few of the initiatives they currently have underway, and I make notes.

"We'd love to work with you at the right time," I chime in when she's done. "This is Dory"—I pull up a brief video of the robot on my computer screen—

"and while we're still developing functionality, here are some of the things she can do."

Both women lean in toward the screen, smiling.

"What do you think, Chris?" The older woman turns to the younger woman at her side.

"It sounds like an amazing project."

"Great. Well"—the woman checks her watch—"I'm afraid I need to jump on another call, but it was a pleasure meeting you, Olivia. Chris will make sure to follow up to email you more information on some of our current projects and partnerships."

"Thank you."

"I've only been with the organization for a few months," Chris says once her boss is gone.

"It's fascinating. I'd love to work with a program like yours when I'm done with school."

"My dad's in engineering. He actually runs a pretty big consulting firm—the one we work with most often."

"Oh! Is that how you got this job?" Her face goes blank and I backtrack. "I didn't mean to imply you didn't deserve it. In my friends and family circles, a lot of people do."

"No, it's fine," she says after a minute. "I got it through a friend. Actually, Dwayne, the VP at my dad's company who made this intro."

"I get it. I mean, I got this introduction from my professor, Dr. Redmond."

Her lips part. "Dr. Who?"

"Redmond. Sawyer Redmond."

Her face goes pale.

What the hell did I say?

Chris looks around her, checking the office door is closed behind her before turning back.

I feel as if I should know what's happening, but it's slippery and my mind can't make the connection. Something is wrong—very wrong.

"How do you know S—Professor Redmond?"

She shifts in her chair, as if she's changed her mind and wishes the door was open so she could make a break for it.

"He was my dad's business partner."

The pieces click together, slowly at first, then faster.

The knot forming in my gut is cold and hard.

"You're the reason Sawyer lost his company."

I'm having trouble reconciling the woman Sawyer painted as a villain with the earnest girl sitting on the other side of the video call.

"He told you?"

I nod, and she presses her lips together.

"I didn't mean to hurt him. I was trying to help

someone else. I never meant for it to get out of control."

My nails dig into my palm, anger over what Sawyer went through challenging my instinctive compassion for another woman. One who, until a minute ago, I was inclined to like very much.

"He put his entire soul into creating that company, and your words took it away from him."

"He got a settlement."

The control inside me cracks. "You think it's the same? He had a hard life before he was our age. Everyone rejected him. Then he built this one thing on his own merit, and now each person who signed onto that venture thinks horrible things about him. Not only that, but the accusations followed him to Russell, and then..."

I trail off. It's not her fault Sawyer and I were discovered, or that we chose to do something against the rules. That's on us.

"I'm sorry," she says quietly. "I never knew him well. But love makes you do crazy things. I guess you're lucky to have it."

"Love doesn't justify hurting other people. Especially when they haven't done anything to hurt you."

When I hang up, I stare at the blank computer screen for a long time.

16

SAWYER

She's pissed about my visit to her mom.

I could've anticipated it. But I'm a shoot first, ask questions later man.

It's not as if I was betraying her by doing it. I felt like a good man and I wanted to do something else good.

If she knew what her mom did for her...

But I can't tell her. I promised.

So I'm stuck playing the bad guy again, an envelope of cash stashed in my sock drawer.

I wanted to tell Olivia's mom to keep it, that I can provide for Olivia. I wouldn't be worthy if I let something as stupid as money come between her and her dreams.

Except I sensed that her mom needed to help more than Olivia needed the assistance.

I'm starting to figure that out. What it feels like to support another person, to feel compelled to do it. Like you can't sleep or eat or look yourself in the mirror if you don't.

Watching Olivia and the kids on stage, tromping around with their penguin hats, made me think of the ones at the NFL game.

They were so damned happy.

A simple thing, to be included. To feel as if another person cares enough to go out of their way for you.

It would've made me happy at that age.

Still, I could've had it worse. My dad could've gone through with what he planned in the letter I found before the holidays and got rid of me entirely.

"Sawyer Redmond. How lovely to see you."

I pocket my phone as a figure advances down the hall toward me.

The short, graying woman with a tailored black suit and pearls is familiar though I haven't seen her in twenty years.

"Marcia. Thank you for meeting me at the end of your workday."

Her kind eyes and lined face beam back at me. "No problem. I finished presenting at a city council meeting down the street, so it was easy to stop by the office. To what do I owe the honor?"

"I want to talk about getting involved in the community."

She gestures toward her office door and I follow her inside. It's simple, an oversized surplus desk and a sofa and chairs opposite.

"Financially?" She takes a chair and I claim the sofa, leaning back.

"I already give to a number of causes in the city. I thought it could be something more…" I shrug. "Personal."

I'm here for a few more months. Might as well try to make a difference.

I tell her about the Big Brothers, Big Sisters box at the football game.

She leans in. "I'm so pleased to hear that. I can think of a number of organizations locally we interface with that could provide the sort of structure you're looking for. You're a shining example, and there are lots of young people in the community who would benefit from your experience."

"I appreciate your confidence."

"The moment Albert came in wanting to foster you, I had a good feeling about your future."

My hand clenches. The letter I found in my father's office, saying he changed his mind about adopting me and wanted to send me back, comes back full force. Other things have been more pressing lately but this one lurks in the corners of my mind.

"I have a hard time imagining he was ever enthused about being a foster parent. Or any kind of parent."

"Are you kidding? He wanted it. I can always tell because they're nervous. They don't want to screw up. In fact, I probably shouldn't say this, but he's passed so I think it's okay." She uncrosses and recrosses her legs. "He wanted to know everything about you. Every home you'd been in. We gave him what information we could, the things you'd told us and what the families reported. We knew you liked to build things, and that it wasn't always welcome. He promised that would be allowed."

That much is true, I suppose. He always provided lots to stimulate my creativity.

"He also berated me."

"Your mother ignored you." Her eyes soften. "I'm not trying to defend him, but he knew that, too. Attention is better than neglect. Sometimes we have a hard time translating wanting the best for someone into how to help them."

The man Olivia talks about is different from the one I knew—he offered help freely, shared ideas and books and games with students. He cared about their futures, created detailed teaching notes and creative new exercises when as a tenured faculty member, he didn't need to go to the effort.

That wasn't what we had. But it never once occurred to me that it stemmed from lack of skill rather than lack of motivation.

"He used to come to classes when he first took you in," she goes on. "Not the mandatory ones, but extra ones. It was hard for him to find time between teaching classes as a junior faculty member and caring for a child, but he made it work. If only all our foster parents were so devoted."

Lancaster, taking parenting classes? It's impossible to visualize.

But she's looking at me, earnest, and I guess she was around long enough to know.

"I found a letter in his drawer that he asked to bring me back."

"We never received it."

I arch a brow. "You lost it."

"No. He never sent it." She frowns, seeming to collect herself before she speaks again. "Being a new parent is overwhelming. Especially when a child you've just met arrives in your home with their own experiences and traumas. I can't know what was on his mind, of course, but perhaps he wrote that letter and kept it as a reminder of the moments of doubt."

She's saying he wanted me.

I'm not ready to believe it.

But even the slightest possibility has warmth spreading through my chest.

Before I can decide how to respond, my phone blinks with a text.

Cherry: Can we talk?

"Excuse me. I'm afraid I need to go, and you must want to get home." I shift out of my seat. "But let's figure out how to make this happen."

"Of course. I can put you in touch with a couple of executive directors who'd love to meet you. Oh, and Sawyer?"

At the doorway, I turn back.

"Do you have children of your own? It's not mandatory that I know, I'm simply curious." She folds her arms, mouth curving.

"I don't." I lift a shoulder and the way she's looking at me has my mouth twitching too. "Maybe someday."

17

OLIVIA

"Theresa's gone," I say when Sawyer gets to the top of the fire escape. "You could've come in the front."

"Now you tell me?" But he's studying my face, trying to see if I'm still pissed.

"I had a call with the environmental group. Did you know the person I was speaking with?"

I give him her name and he frowns. "No. Should I?"

I help him in through the window. There's a smudge of dirt on his arm.

"There was also a woman named Chris."

He stops halfway through rubbing a hand across his stubbled jaw.

"Christine?"

"Yes. She told me what happened."

He paces the length of my room, gaze fixed on the hardwood floors. "It's in the past, Olivia. And while those weeks and months were excruciating, in the end I can't regret them. Because if I hadn't left..." he stops and cuts a look at me. "I wouldn't have met you."

The earnestness in his tone makes my chest expand. "And I'm grateful for that, too. But she didn't only do it to you, Sawyer. She hurt herself, and others. So many women speak up and *aren't* heard. When something like this happens, everyone loses."

My arms are wrapped around my body, my hands balled into fists, but they loosen as he grabs my waist and tugs me closer.

"I know you're angry I went to see your mother. But I finished at my old offices and I felt like I did one thing right. For once in a long goddamned time, I did something right. I wanted to keep it going."

I chew my lip. "How was dropping by my parents' apartment keeping it going? What did you guys talk about?"

"You." He says it simply. "I told her I would look out for you."

God, it's hard to stay mad at him. "Is that all?"

He hesitates, arousing my suspicion again, but finally nods. "If I were in her shoes, I would want to know someone was looking out for my kid." His brows pull together. "I didn't give her all the details, because hearing the specific ways I like to look out for you wouldn't be comforting, but…"

At my smile, he trails off.

"You want to have kids one day?" I whisper.

"I don't know. Maybe with the right person."

My stomach flips over, but this time, it's a good flip. "Promise me you won't go to my mom directly again."

He turns that over before nodding. "She cares about you."

I shove at his chest. "Okay, this is too weird. You defending my mom—"

"Not defending. There are a lot of ways to show love. That's all I'm saying."

My heart hammers as I glance down at the streak of mud on his shirt. "You're dirty."

"Always."

"This is the fixable kind." My lips twitch. "Let me clean you up. It's the least I can do."

He follows me through my room and out into the kitchen.

"Whoa. You keeping some monster under there?" Sawyer nods to the covered birdcage in the corner.

"Monty. He's sleeping. He sleeps a lot."

"It's a harsh world."

I grin and lead him to the sink, pulling his arm under the faucet. "On second thought, take it off."

"Yes, ma'am."

Sawyer unbuttons his shirt, eyes glinting with heat. I bite my cheek as he strips out of it, the undershirt beneath clinging to cut shoulders and hard abs.

He tosses the fabric at me and I go to work on the stain while he watches.

"There," I say moments later, triumphant. "All better."

"This feels so normal," he comments from behind me.

"You hate it."

"I love it."

I barely have time to turn before he pins me between him and the counter, his hips flush with mine.

"Does watching me do your laundry turn you on?" I breathe. It's hard to argue with the growing arousal pressing against my stomach.

"Everything you do turns me on." He brushes a piece of hair from my face and lowers his lips to my jaw.

"Hey," I start, pulling back. "Do you want to stay for dinner? We could have a normal couple night."

"I'd like that very much." The slow curve of his

lips is the best reward. "What else does a normal couple night involve?"

I hadn't gotten that far.

"Things we would do if you weren't ten years older and my professor. If we'd met some ordinary way."

"You mean you didn't meet Adam at a strip club?" His brows lift, mocking, before he moves closer to nibble at my jaw again.

"Um. No." I smile, looping my arms around his neck. "Our parents were at a social event."

"And you like that he was the golden boy."

"I liked that he was easy." His teeth scrape my skin and I arch closer, wantonly asking for more. "I like that you're not."

"I am easy, Cherry. When it comes to you."

His hands find my ass, cupping me through my yoga pants.

The next second I'm on the counter; he's lifted me up and set me on the edge. His hair falls in his face, a smug grin on his firm lips.

"Wanted you the first time I saw you. I always took these tokens of things in my life—this watch, rocks, other little shit. It was my fucked-up collection. Pretty soon, I wanted to take a piece of you, too."

I reach for my necklace, but he stops me. "No."

"What's so funny?" I ask when his eyes dance. "I want to give you something of mine."

"Sweetheart, the piece of you I'm taking can't be seen."

His mouth claims mine, and I thread my fingers in his hair.

When he grips my hips, pulling me to rub harder on him, I lean back to give his hungry mouth access.

But I push him away, because if we start this, it'll be a long time before we stop. "I promised to make you dinner."

"You are dinner."

I pull my shirt back up and shift out, dropping to the floor. "But I have pasta. And marinara sauce. And cheese." I play my trump card, but Sawyer looks at me like I'm cute and a little insane.

"You expect me to pass you up for…cheese?"

I laugh. "It's really good cheese."

"It fucking better be."

I set to work on dinner, and he helps.

We put on music and laugh and dance. We make out a little but when he tries to take it further, I duck out of his arms.

Kat and Jules and I sometimes cooked together, but it was rare because of busy school schedules. Before that, I never cooked at home.

This, with Sawyer? It's bliss.

Within minutes, the sauce is simmering happily on the stove and I'm feeling quite accomplished. "Can you get me a wooden spoon?"

Sawyer goes through the drawers, eventually finding one. But when I reach for it, he holds it back, a glint in his eyes.

"You've been telling me what to do for half an hour."

"Are you man enough to take orders from a woman?"

"Mm-hmm. But there's got to be a reversal at some point."

"The reward for not being a misogynistic asshole is that you get to eat my sauce."

He checks the timer. "Yeah, I'm not waiting fifteen minutes to eat your sauce. Bend over."

My jaw drops. "What happened to normal couple stuff?"

"This is normal couple stuff, Cherry. Hands on the counter."

The constant buzz of arousal that's been present since he showed up intensifies, settling into an electric current between my thighs.

We haven't done anything like this since the night of Black Build, when he pulled me upstairs after his open house and I sucked him off and he took me from behind.

The sex the other night was amazing, but I also love Sawyer when he takes charge. I love the way he gets me out of my head, makes me feel alive the way only he can.

So I place both hands on the counter.

He drags my hips where he wants them, then yanks my pants down my thighs with one hand.

What he finds beneath my clothes has him groaning. "Commando?"

"Laundry day."

"Or you knew I was coming over. Show me that ass, Olivia. I'm going to spank you red."

An excited flush crawls up my face as I glance back at him over my shoulder.

He's gorgeous like this—commanding and playful at the same time, his hair wild around his face, his shoulders bare beneath the undershirt and his jaw flexing with intent.

But even when he thinks he's in control, I can mess with him.

I arch my back, a slow move that leaves my hips tilted up and elicits a groan from Sawyer.

"You know, I can never decide what part of you I like best."

"My brain. The correct answer is my—AH!"

I gasp at the sting on my skin as the spoon comes down.

The pain is sharp, cutting into the pleasure of being stretched out like this under his gaze.

Okay, he's having a little too much fun.

"You were a brat after I got back from New York," he murmurs as if hearing my thoughts.

"Because you were out of line talking to my mom. Couples fight," I remind him.

"But you weren't fighting fair."

The wood comes down on my ass, the other side this time, and I bite down on my tongue.

"Same with when you took off during exams," he continues. "You shut down on me. I love you, Olivia, but if this thing with us is going to work, we've got to communicate."

The little thrill that seems to accompany each time he says those three words fades into disbelief as I process the rest of them.

Did Sawyer just say that?

When I twist back again, I'm sure of it. He's studying me with a look that's both hungry and intent.

And he's waiting for my answer.

Now that I know he's been abandoned by his mom and had other people turn his back on him, I don't ever want to hurt him that way.

"Okay. I won't push you away without talking about it."

"Good." Relief edges into his expression, and a wicked gleam enters his eye. "To make sure you remember, I'm going to make you as red as that sauce. Don't worry...I promise you'll be dripping in no time."

He follows through.

The wooden implement leaves my skin stinging, but it also heightens my awareness of what we're doing, and anticipation for what we're about to do.

It's better than the last time we did this because he's not truly trying to punish me. After each swat, his hand runs my skin, soothing the pain away.

"She's wet." Sawyer's hand slips between my legs, testing and teasing. "What do you think, should you bring this to the dinner table? Or take care of it first?"

"You better take care of it," I gripe.

I hear the sound of his zipper. My back is stiff from holding this position, but there's not enough money in the world to get me to move when I feel the head of his thick cock press against me.

"Oh shit." Both my elbows brace on the counter as he sinks inside me.

"I think I'm almost ready to forgive you for shutting me out," he groans.

"Almost?" I pant. "I could draw a dick on your face with permanent marker and you'd forgive me right now."

He laughs as his hands find my breasts, impatiently shoving up my bra to squeeze my flesh while he rocks into me.

He fits me as tight as the first time, only now he knows my body, how to make me writhe and moan.

He knows what rhythm drives me crazy. How hard to tug my nipples and when to rub my clit when I'm about to come.

And given all the anticipation, it doesn't take much.

"Tell me you're close."

"I'm close," I choke out.

Pleasure tightens into an unstable molten core, one that throbs and then shatters and drags me along with it.

"Ohmigod, Sawyer... Yes, I'm coming!"

Ecstasy chases along my nerves, washing over me in a wave.

When my aftershocks subside, he lets himself come on a long groan. His hips bruise mine, his release spilling into me in endless streams.

I'm face-first in the counter when the timer beeps and Sawyer's hot breath puffs at my ear.

"I guess the sauce is ready."

"Long night?" Theresa calls from the dinette when I stick my head out of my room the next morning.

I rub my sleepy eyes and adjust my pajama top, my muscles complaining. "Um, kind of. When did you get back? I didn't hear you come in."

"Just now." She smiles, sipping a coffee at the table as she takes in my appearance. "Anything in particular you got up to?"

Well, I made dinner with my professor-turned-lover. He spanked me right over there and then we ate the best food and laughed until we cried. And also, we might have broken the bed. The second time, if not the first.

My attention falls to the counter. The dishes are washed and dried on a cloth next to the sink.

Did Sawyer do these before he left this morning?

Gratitude about him cleaning up clashes with guilt over having him stay the night.

"I had a guy over. I'm sorry. But it wasn't a random hookup, he's my boyfriend. And he's actually been to the studio before dropping off his friend's kid. So I swear he's not a creeper."

Theresa folds her arms but there's a smile on her lips.

"You knew?" My mouth falls open.

My boss turns toward the birdcage in the corner. "Monty?"

The parrot chirps on his peg. *"Gonna spank you. Gonna spank you."*

I press a hand to my cheek and squeeze my eyes shut.

It's so embarrassing. "Please don't kick me out. I'll make it up to you."

The sound of chuckling makes me force my eyes open again. Theresa's amused, not angry. "You will make it up to me. I need you at Velvet. It's Ladies' Night."

18

OLIVIA

"This is what Ladies' Night means?" I call over the noise.

Theresa answers with a wink from across the bar at Velvet.

Today was a whirlwind. After last night with Sawyer, I spent today sharing what I learned from the non-profit with the team and coming up with extra changes to make to Dory. Madison, Royce, Adam, and I worked in the lab for hours.

Now, I'd love to unwind. Instead of falling into bed, which would feel good after all the hours I've been pulling, I strapped myself into high heels.

I can't serve alcohol, but I'm helping make sure people have waters. I'm dressed in black shorts and heels and a white dress shirt.

When Kat and Jules found out I was coming back to Velvet, they insisted on coming.

Repentant Asshole: Be there soon. I'm bringing the guys.

"Shit," I blurt as the first male stripper takes the stage.

"What's wrong?" Kat asks, and I show her the text.

Jules leans over. "Who are the guys?"

"Other profs from Sawyer's street."

Kat cringes. "How many? Please tell me they're not all seventy."

A few minutes later, a string of guys comes in the door and we have our answer.

I wave and the guys head this way.

Sawyer's in the middle in a dark jacket and jeans, his hair tied back.

On one side is Daniel, in a dress shirt and long coat, his black hair styled. On the other side are two other guys, one with a tattoo snaking up around his neck who introduced himself as Zander, and another preppy one named Ricardo.

It's a lot to take in. Kat in particular looks impressed.

"I got a babysitter for this?" Daniel demands, cutting a look at the stage.

"No takebacks, gentlemen."

Sawyer jingles his keys. "I'm driving, and you did get a babysitter so you might as well enjoy this."

"Unlikely."

Kat snorts and he cuts her a frown.

"You're shortsighted," Kat calls.

"How's that?"

"You're looking at one dude on the stage. Instead" —she takes his shoulders and turns him to face the crowd—"of the entire audience of hungry women. It's called vision, friend. Get some."

Her hands linger on his shoulders and I see his jaw tighten before she melts away, grabbing Jules. "I've got ones."

"These are your friends?" Zander, the tatted guy, asks.

"Mm-hmm. You like?" I glance at Daniel.

"I think I need a drink."

"I'm not a server, but I can flag Troy down..." I trail off. "You know what? I'll send him over. You look like you could use it."

The music is great, and the night is super popular

so far. The place is nearly full and the guys on stage are awesome.

After I send the bartender over and refill my tray of waters, I hand them out, swaying my hips to the music.

I'm so fucking happy right now.

When I'm over by the booths, someone catches my hand. I grab for my tray before it flies to the floor.

Sawyer tugs me against him behind the booths. "Hi."

"Hi, you. You look sexy with your hair like that."

"You look sexy with your legs like that. Makes me think about them wrapped around my hips."

I bite my lip. "Wanna try? We had a lot of fun last time."

The memory of me stripping for him and having sex on a chair before we went back to his place is burned into my mind forever.

The smoldering expression on his face says he hasn't forgotten either.

"This time I wouldn't let you off near as easy," he murmurs in my ear.

"You kept me up all night."

"But I let you take the shoes off."

I shove at his chest.

"You could've given us a heads-up it was guys on stage," he drawls.

"That would have been no fun at all."

"You're right. And these guys probably wouldn't have come. Though now I understand why Ric's wife didn't mind him coming."

I cast a look at the guys, the one in question sipping a drink and laughing at his friends, the rest of whom have found women to flirt with. It's one big party, and I love every second of it.

"I almost wish Madison and Royce and Adam were here. Almost," I go on at Sawyer's look. "Royce fell asleep in lab today, and Adam's coach was blowing up his phone."

"The team needs a break."

"We'll have one, after finals. Dory needs to work, and after my call with the environmental group, we have lots more fixes to make. And we only have a month to make them." I take a deep breath and he narrows his gaze.

"Is he always this awkward?" Kat asks, slinging an arm around my neck and another around Sawyer's as she nods to Daniel.

"Give the guy a break. He's been raising Andy on his own."

Kat frowns, her gaze lingering on the guys. "So you're saying he needs to get laid."

"How did she get that from what I said?" Sawyer asks, bewildered, while I laugh.

"She's Kat."

My friend stops in front of Daniel, pressing up on her heels to cup her hands at his ear and shout over the music.

He listens, then shouts back.

"You got any moves, Professor?" I ask, swaying my hips as the next guy takes the stage.

"I think you know."

"But anything I haven't seen."

He drags my hips against him. "Cherry, I have all kinds of moves you haven't seen. I'm just biding my time so I don't scare you away."

The promise in his voice is almost as addictive as the expression on his face.

"I'm really glad you came tonight." I can't stop my grin.

"If you thought I'd bail on you over this, you have no idea how much I love you."

My heart melts and I press a kiss to his mouth.

Theresa hollers from the bar and, reluctant, I pull away. "Duty calls."

I go refill my tray of waters. "This isn't BYO thirst trap, Olivia," she chides, but she's grinning.

"I can't help it. He's hot."

We dance and the crowd drinks and I help keep everyone hydrated.

Sawyer hangs out with his guys and my girlfriends, and after a while I run into Daniel on the way from the bathroom.

"You hanging in?" I ask him.

"It's the most fun I've ever had around mostly-naked men," he concedes, and I laugh. "So I know I came off harsh that night by the studio…"

"It's okay. You were trying to protect him."

Daniel frowns. "I want him to be happy. God knows he deserves it after everything he's been through. But be aware of the choice you're making. I get that you're in love. I've been there, Liv. Trust me. Sawyer's single-minded but I know you think about these things. What are you doing after this semester? He's hell-bent on getting you back into school, so what then? What about after he leaves Russell?"

My throat dries.

"I don't want to kill your buzz. But life has plans even when you don't, so it's better to get ahead of it."

19

SAWYER

"Betty, I need a card to charge this trip to."

She looks up over her desk. "What trip?"

"Las Vegas," I deadpan. "I'll give them the dean's name, book the penthouse, and max out the card while wearing a Russell U sweatshirt."

She cackles with laughter. "Just because you got me my new favorite hat doesn't mean I'll let you away with that." She nods to the corner of her desk, where the souvenir I brought her from the NFL game with the guys is proudly displayed.

Olivia said they need a break, and she's right. The lab hours they've been logging have been strenuous. I've spent at least an hour a day working with them, reviewing progress, offering assistance and insights to try to help them and stretch them at the same time. But we can't afford to let off the gas either.

So I came up with a solution that satisfies both.

"I'm taking the Stars team to Myrtle Beach for the weekend to test Dory. There's supposed to be a budget for this kind of thing." Except for Olivia's portion, which I'll pay.

"There's supposed to be. But there isn't."

Suspicion streaks through me. I wouldn't hesitate to pay for the entire trip myself, except there's clearly budget for this somewhere in the department. Olivia donated my dad's money, for fuck's sake.

"Screw it, I'm putting the travel on the university's card. If the dean loses his temper, you can send him my way."

"All right. As for a card, your dad had one. It should be in his desk."

"I've cleaned out his desk. There's nothing there."

"What about his Go set?" she asks, rounding the desk and starting toward my office. "There was a drawer in the bottom."

I push the door wide and wait for her to go in first. "He can't keep running the department this way, Betty. It's gone on too long."

"Someone's going to break, but it won't be him." Betty sighs. "I've been working nights and weekends for no extra pay. But since what happened with Livvy's expulsion, I can't stand the man."

"What did he have to do with that?" The hairs on my neck rise.

It was supposed to have been decided by the committee, signed off by the vice provost.

"He was personally embarrassed by the revelation about her father. Called the man to thank him, only to realize he'd been duped."

My hands form fists and I remember Olivia's mother's words about men in charge making decisions.

"Would you do something to help me? It would be a risk, but I promise I will have your back."

She shakes her head slowly. "Sawyer, I can't. I've been here twenty-five years. I don't want to put my retirement in jeopardy."

And there's the problem. People have built their futures on this institution, trusting it will be there for them after their loyal service.

As much as I want to push, I couldn't live with myself costing this woman—who's always been there for me, for my father, every student in need—her hard-won security.

Betty reaches for the game, jostling the drawer.

"There's the card." She hands it to me. "And if

you max it out, that's on you." Her lips twitch. "But I would like to see his face if you do."

She departs and I pull out my phone.

Sawyer: Pack your bags. We're going on a weekend trip.

Dots appear almost immediately.

Cherry: Are you going to tell me where? And what I should pack?

Sawyer: We're bringing Adam.

Cherry: ?!?!?!

Sawyer: And Madison and Royce and Dory.

The phone jumps in my hand and I hit answer.

"Now you've got me. I'm in between teaching

dance classes, but this can't wait. What are we doing?"

My lips curve as I hold up the black credit card. "We're going to put this project to the test. And you can pack a bathing suit."

"Because we're going swimming or you want to see me in as few clothes as possible?"

"Both."

When we arrive at the airport in South Carolina, the weather is considerably warmer than when we left.

"Damn, Redmond, we couldn't charter a plane?" Royce says for the millionth time since takeoff. We took economy, which I haven't done in years. My legs are cramped and the echo of a baby crying still rings in my ears.

"I didn't realize your name was Drake. Department funding covered commercial flights only. And it's Professor Redmond," I remind him.

Madison rolls her bag a few feet behind us. "Is that what she calls you?"

"She calls me whatever the fuck she wants." I toss my jacket over one shoulder and thread my fingers through Olivia's as we head away from the gate.

I'm not her professor and we're far from Russell,

and anyone who would turn us in would be as screwed as we would.

"Everyone needs to get checked in," I say as we collect our bags. "Dory will be delivered right to the shore where we've arranged to test. There's surveillance equipment available from the Coast Guard that we can connect to monitor the robot's performance on tasks we've set up, plus maneuverability."

"Still can't believe you did this," Olivia murmurs, squeezing my hand.

"This matters." I squeeze back.

We head to the hotel I booked.

"I have four rooms listed," the woman at check-in says as she holds out keycards. "Is that correct?"

Madison and Royce each reach for one, leaving two left.

I take one key, and Olivia slides the other across to Adam.

It was simplest for me to pay for her flight—it didn't feel right to put her on department money—but she's rooming with me.

"We'll need to work at high tide. That's in ninety minutes." I check my watch.

"Meet down here in half an hour?" Madison asks.

"Done." Olivia nods.

We take our bags upstairs, Madison and Royce teasing each other. Adam's quiet.

"Give me a sec," I say to Olivia once we get up to our room. She shoots me a questioning look, but I nod as I duck out to see Adam.

"Everything okay?"

"Super," he says dryly. "You're shacking up with my girlfriend." He looks at me like he wants to kill me.

I jerk my head toward the stairwell and he follows me out to the silent, fluorescent-lit landing.

"You're right, it's fucked up." His jaw slackens in surprise. "I shouldn't have dated a student. You shouldn't have cheated on her. Her parents shouldn't have pressured her every day of her life. Yours should support you playing basketball or whatever you want to do. My dad shouldn't have been an asshole to me, and my mom shouldn't have died. But that's life. None of us do it perfectly."

He's quiet. Too quiet.

"When you said this mattered more to me than I knew, you were right," I hear myself go on. "But you were wrong to say it didn't matter to you. Or Olivia. Or Madison. There are moments in your life that you have a chance to be better than you are. To do things that are hard, even if you're not sure you can. That's why we do them. Because they're hard. Because we might fail. And it's not only a professional success or failure. Every choice you make turns you into the person you are. You just need to decide what kind of person you want to be."

Adam leans over the railing, peering down at the endless flights of stairs below. I don't know if he's listening or tuning me out.

"That video of Liv I sent to Madison...that was a bad move."

My spine stiffens, my hands clenching into fists as anger boils through me.

She didn't tell me Adam was the one to spread the video. Probably didn't want me holding her ex's head in front of one of the dual props on the plane earlier.

I force myself to reach for the door handle. "Get ready. We'll meet you in a few minutes."

When I get back to our room, Olivia's in the bathroom so I change and prepare.

"Everything good?" she asks when she emerges.

"Mm-hmm." I brush my lips across hers.

I'm going to kill one of my students. But no big.

Her gaze flicks to the bed with the metal posts. "It's a beautiful room. How old do you think these are?" She trails a finger over the posts, and I'm suddenly more aware of her than my simmering rage.

"Dunno. How thick do you think the walls are?"

I back her into the wall, her softness calling to me.

My hands slide down to grab her ass, her curves filling my palms.

"We have to go," she breathes.

"Yeah. But later, you're mine."

"Adam's sleeping on the other side. Being loud would be petty."

"Only if we're doing it for him. We'd be doing it despite him."

Her smile lights up the entire damn room.

"Who's driving?" I call into the breeze as we pile into the rented thirty-foot fishing boat at the port.

"Me. I play the most video games." Adam grabs for the controls.

The boat's captain takes us away from the shore a few hundred feet. Once we're out, we lift Dory over the side.

"Here goes nothing," Olivia breathes.

"It feels like we're sending our baby out to sea." Madison laughs, but it's nerves.

"She'll come back."

"Fucking better. This thing is my future." Royce

shifts against the side of the boat, pulling his jacket around him.

The bot starts to descend into the water, disappearing beneath the surface.

We're blind.

Now the only way to monitor Dory is through the screen Madison opens on her tablet.

"The water's a lot rougher than we expected," Adam says a few minutes later, grimacing.

Royce shakes his head. "It won't be for the competition."

The robot appears on the radar, emitting a signal as Adam guides it through the water.

Our Coast Guard partners have helped us set out a few specific challenges for Dory to tackle.

"First up, there's the navigation challenge," Olivia reads off the page.

Adam steers Dory through sets of beacons on the bottom.

"So far so good. Now documentation."

Madison works the camera remotely. "That should be it."

"Great. Sample collection."

This is the part where Dory is supposed to scoop sand from the bottom and seal it in a compartment to bring above the surface.

But Adam frowns.

"What's wrong?" Olivia demands.

"Just having trouble with the angle. I can get it better this way." He works the controls.

The screen shows the bot's movements. "Adam, there's too much resistance," I say. "Find another spot."

"It'll be fine." He grits his teeth and tries again.

"Adam—"

"Shit!" He presses a button once. Twice. A bunch of times in quick succession. "She won't come back up. She's stuck."

"What do you mean stuck?" Royce demands.

"Stuck. Won't move forward. Won't come back up. Immobile. Fucking stuck—"

"Dammit!" My teeth grind together as I glare at the kid. "We didn't need to get on a plane and fly down here for you to bury the thing at the bottom of the ocean."

Madison's eyes widen and Royce covers his face with both hands. Adam looks around, defensive until reality seems to catch up to him.

"It's okay. I'll go get it," Adam says, rising and stripping off his life jacket.

"Are you sure?" Olivia's face is concerned.

"Yeah. It's my fault she got stuck."

"This was a bad idea," Royce mutters when Adam dives in. Olivia and Madison exchange a look.

"It's not that deep. Twenty feet, max."

Olivia wraps her arms around her.

The engine starts up and all our heads whip toward the helm of the boat, where the captain sits behind his steering wheel.

"Hey!" I shout, waving my arms. "Cut the engine."

"Our time's up. We have to go back."

"One of my kids has gone in."

It takes a minute for him to understand and comply. When I turn back to point at my team, only Madison and Royce stand peering over the side of the boat.

My heart drops through my feet. I'm next to them in three strides.

"What the fuck happened?"

Madison grips the edge. "She just went over."

Water laps the side of the boat, harmless ripples turned sinister.

Memories slam into me.

Dark, rippling water.

The feeling of terror.

The kind of loneliness I couldn't have known would only get worse.

No.

This isn't happening.

I'm tearing off my own life jacket and preparing

to dive in when two heads appear over the side. One has short light hair, the other longer and dark.

Madison and Royce are already moving to the back of the boat and lowering the ladder.

I haul them both up, Olivia first, then Adam.

They collapse on the deck, soaked and panting.

Wet clothes cling to their bodies. Olivia's hair is plastered to her face.

She coughs up water and I lean her forward, hitting her back to help. When she lifts a hand to assure me she's fine, I force myself to turn to Adam.

He's on his back staring up at the sky.

It's one thing for me to demand excellence, but this isn't on Adam. These students are here under my supervision, and it's a thousand times worse than the car crash during Black Build. He's my responsibility.

"Turn over," I grunt, helping to shift him.

"Where's Dory?"

His voice is rough and weak.

"Don't worry about it."

"But—"

"I'll have the Coast Guard drag the floor and get her back. We're done here," I inform the captain when he comes over to check on us.

Olivia coughs. "But we didn't finish testing—"

"We're done."

20

OLIVIA

"Take a bath and I'll get you checked over properly," Sawyer bites out the second we're inside the hotel room.

"It's fine," I assure him. "No one got hurt. And we'll get Dory back."

He yanks on his hair, pacing the room. "This is my fault. I brought you all here."

"I went in after Adam. I was always the better swimmer. Nothing would've happened. You and Madison and Royce were there."

When he turns back to me, his face is white. "The last time I saw someone go in she didn't come out."

His mom.

Horror washes over me.

I didn't think about it earlier. All I focused on was getting Dory back.

Now, I see Sawyer's pain, his fear, his grief.

"I don't want to lose you." His voice is so low I can barely hear it.

My chest expands, my heart thudding against my ribs. "You won't. I'm not going anywhere."

I've seen Sawyer angry, and jealous, and betrayed. I've never seen him lost.

But for the first time, I can imagine what he must have looked like as a child, and felt like. Realizing he was utterly alone in the world.

I'm so caught up, it takes a moment to recognize the rumbling of my stomach.

"Unless I starve to death. Did you say something about a dinner reservation?"

Thirty minutes later, we're walking along the boardwalk and he's holding my hand, as if he's still half afraid I'll vanish any second.

The restaurant is all white clapboard with warm, inviting lights. We're shown to a table near the back of the restaurant, with a view of the water through huge windows.

I glance at the menu with a smile. "You can put ketchup on anything here."

Sawyer shudders. "They'll forcibly remove you."

I lean in. "In that case... I dare you."

His admiring grin is all I need.

We get a bottle of wine. I order swordfish and he gets surf and turf.

"I'll take you for dinner every night if it makes you smile like this," he says when our wine arrives.

"Where else would you take me for dinner?"

"Anywhere you fucking want."

I take a sip, the light bubbles playing on my tongue. "I received the reference letters you arranged."

"You did?"

I nod. "Hopefully, I can get into Columbia, which means another two years. What do you want to do?"

"Easy. Tate and I will start the business like we planned."

"What if Russell asks you to stay permanently? What if they make you an offer you can't refuse?"

He laughs. "I'm not a professor, Olivia, and the university knows that. They want me to see Stars through. I stayed because I wanted to get you back into school. Yes, it felt good to be wanted. But it's not a long term fit. I won't be happy teaching when I could be working in industry on cutting edge projects."

"What if they beg you? It could happen," I insist.

"Then I'll say no. I don't belong there. It was always meant to be temporary."

The dismissive way he says it makes my chest twinge.

He's talking about school, not us. It's stupid that those words make me worry.

When dinner comes, I ask for ketchup, then offer it to him when he arrives.

"Absolutely not," he decides, biting into his steak.

I grin, mischievous. "I could stick it in my purse. Save it for later. You could lick it off me."

His fork freezes halfway to his mouth. "I'm incredibly aroused."

"You're a complicated man."

Dinner is delicious, and we talk about everything from new shows on streaming to favorite places in New York to countries we've traveled to or wished we had.

When we've nearly finished our meals, I dab my mouth with a napkin. "You're older. You've done a lot more than me."

He looks up with surprise. "Does it bother you?"

"Sometimes."

Sawyer shifts back in his seat, his handsome face unusually thoughtful. "Experience is the best teacher, but you're a better student than I am. The last six months I feel like I'm learning every day."

My heart expands. I love him so damn much I can barely contain the feeling.

"Dessert?" he asks after our plates are cleared.

The wine is going to my head, the second glass wreaking havoc.

"I thought I was dessert."

Sawyer hands over his credit card without breaking my gaze.

We hurry out of there and into the cab.

The entire way back it's hard to keep focused.

When we return to the hotel, we trip up the stairs.

"Are you drunk?"

"Just tipsy."

"There's a protocol for that." He grabs me and lifts me over his shoulder.

"This is very inelegant, Professor Redmond," I mumble, even as I sniff the back of his clothes.

"Disagree. The view from here is extremely appealing."

We get down the hall and Sawyer swipes the card over the door and holds it open; I'm already throbbing with anticipation.

Inside, he takes a seat on the end of the bed to study me. The slow perusal starts at my feet, clad in high heels, runs up my legs, and lingers on my hips, my breasts, before finding my face.

"Remember when you took me to the ballet and

the aquarium?" I murmur. "It felt as if we were running off together."

"It feels like that still. I'd follow you anywhere, Olivia."

The reverence on his face, the intention in his voice, steals my breath.

It's quiet in here, only the two of us and the quiet sound from the minibar running.

I step closer, and his hands find my hips. He tries to tug me into his lap, but I resist.

"When you asked me to move to New York with you, I said no because I didn't want to leave things behind but also because I was scared." I swallow. "I don't want to be scared anymore, Sawyer. I just want to love you."

He's looking up at me. Just the right angle to see his eyes spark with disbelief, his nostrils flare. "Say it again."

"I've loved you since you took me to the aquarium. Since you made me peanut butter sandwiches after homecoming. Since you kissed me in a parking lot and made me feel like my life was beginning instead of ending."

He doesn't move, as if he's worried he'll shatter the moment between us.

Eventually he reaches for my waist, pulling me

close. But instead of kissing me, he just shifts forward, leaning his forehead against me.

"I've imagined you saying that. It's better in real life," he whispers against my stomach.

I hold him there, my fingers playing in his hair as emotions collide inside me like the waves that battered the boat.

"When I came back this semester," I begin, "you were careful with me. You're still careful with me." Even when we mess around, when we had sex in the kitchen, it was light and fun. It felt as if Sawyer was guarding part of himself he didn't want to let out. "I want you to stop."

Stop treating me like I'm fragile, like saying or doing the wrong thing will send me running.

At first, I'm not sure he's heard me.

But I can feel the moment everything changes.

He pulls back an inch, raising dark eyes to meet mine.

A shiver runs through me as he unfastens the button on one cuff.

Then the other.

Sawyer rolls up his shirtsleeves before shoving both hands through his hair, as if he refuses to have anything—even a few wayward strands—between us.

"Take off the dress."

His words are low and silky smooth.

He's looking at me as if the world has gone to sleep and it's the two of us alone in the universe.

I reach behind me, my fingers slipping on the zipper.

When the fabric slips over my hips and drops to the floor, the only sign of its effect is the way his throat bobs.

I'm standing in a pink lace bra and no panties.

"Are you going to touch me?" I ask.

"I am touching you."

I'm tempted to shift on my feet, but his attention is exquisite. He drinks me in and it's raw, blatant.

Like he wants to love me and ruin me at once.

"You tried so damned hard to be perfect for everyone else, but you know what I thought when I saw you that first night?" he murmurs. "A woman who wanted permission to be herself. I can't give you permission to go after your dreams. All I can do is watch with admiration as you do."

My heart is thudding so loud it's incredible it doesn't drown out his words.

Finally he rises, still dressed in his button-down shirt and pants and dress shoes.

When he wraps his arms around me, the fabric rubs at my pointed nipples, my bare back. His rough hand palms my ass.

I gasp. It feels so good to be held by him like this.

"This is what you want." He's reminding me, or asking.

Either way I nod, my lips tingling as they brush his shirt.

He reaches up to thread his fingers in my hair, turning my head to face the door.

There's a mirror on the back.

I lose my breath as I soak in the image reflected in it.

In it, I'm naked and he's dressed, he's big and I'm small, he's wrapped around me as if I'm his prized possession.

"Keep watching."

He drops to his knees, spreading my legs, revealing where I'm already aching for him.

"Show me how wet you are."

There's no room for nerves, his voice and the thick air between us crowd them out.

I reach down and part my slick skin and he groans his approval.

"Tell me you're mine."

I catch sight of myself in the mirror moments before he descends, his lips closing over my clit.

"I'm yours," I pant, my hand fisting in his hair.

My back bows as I arch into his tongue.

His fingers slip inside, first one and then two, as if he's intending to prove his claim.

And he does.

He owns me with his touch, his lips, his confidence.

He pulls back before I can come, lifting me and carrying me back toward the bed.

I reach for his shirt, making quick work of the buttons while his hands are occupied. I spread the fabric, revealing his gorgeous chest and abs.

More.

His belt is next, and I shove at his pants and briefs, struggling with the straining outline of his thick cock.

I win.

When he lays me down beneath him, he grabs my wrists and lifts them over my head.

"I need to touch you." I pout.

"I want to take care of you." He unfastens his watch, setting it on the bed next to my head.

"This a race?" I tease.

"The opposite, actually."

He unclasps my necklace next and lays it on the other side.

What is he about to do?

I'm flushed and breathless and he really does seem as if he's not in a hurry.

Finally, he takes my wrist and lifts it to one of the metal bedposts, where he secures it with his watch.

His eyes gleam as he sees the second I realize what he's doing.

Then he takes my other wrist and fastens it too, looping my necklace twice around.

"Don't pull," he warns, stroking a thumb over my wrist. "I don't want you to hurt yourself. Can you do that?"

I nod, biting my lip.

He gets off the bed and finds a pair of my panties, looping them inside the metal chain so it's not pinching my wrist.

Sawyer Redmond is fucking beautiful like this. A little terrifying, and I feel like a princess tied up before a monster.

But he's my monster.

"I realized something recently," he says.

He starts down my body, raining kisses on my throat, down to my breasts.

"As human beings, we think that all we want is freedom..."

I arch under him, my wrists tugging lightly before I remember I can't use my hands.

"...The ability to do what we wish without answering to anyone."

I'm at a disadvantage. I can't move, can't stop him,

can't tell him it's too much except with my lips and body.

"But that's an illusion. We want constraints—people, commitments, obligations—but we want constraints that care."

My first test comes when his tongue swirls around my nipple. I arch my hips, rubbing against his cock. He sucks harder, enough to cause a sharp little pain.

"Oh!"

His gaze flicks to mine, and whatever he sees there reassures him because he goes to the other side, doing the same there.

The light pain makes the throbbing at my core deeper, sweeter.

"You're going to be so ready for me."

"I'm ready now," I complain, arching my hips.

He lifts a brow as he rubs me with his thumb and forefinger, making me gasp and writhe. "I don't think you're wet enough."

Except when he pulls back, both his digits are glistening. He sucks me off his thumb, then offers me his finger.

I open my mouth and close around him, my tongue swirling. It's so hot, and watching him watch me sets me on fire.

"I'm going to slide in so deep, you'll never get me

out."

Sawyer's possessive grin lingers in my mind after he goes back to his work.

He's thorough with his touch, teasing and torturing me.

When he shifts over me, pressing his cock against my slit, I moan.

He sinks inside, stretching and filling me.

I gasp, my elbows flexing and my eyes squeezing shut as I try to let him in.

"That's it, sweetheart. I love how you take me." His praise stokes the fire even as it soothes me. "I might be inside you, but trust me—you're in me, too."

Soon I'm arching to meet him, chasing his touch with my hips.

He ties me down and takes care of me in a way only Sawyer could.

It's possessive and protective.

For the second time today, I'm drowning. This time, I don't want to come up for air.

21

SAWYER

Campus is bright on the cusp of February. I've never enjoyed winter, but as I wrap my coat around me and head across the plowed paths to the engineering building, I have a legitimate bounce in my stride.

Until snow hits my head and I look up to see students guiltily exchange a look.

"Sorry, Professor Redmond."

"Practice before you try out for baseball, yeah?"

"Promise."

I tug at my collar but the snow doesn't evaporate as I head toward the engineering building.

I'm in a good mood.

Possibly thanks to Olivia.

On the boat in Myrtle Beach, I was terrified of losing her.

It wasn't until she was under me that I could take a steadying breath.

Until she told me she loved me.

I can't remember the last time anyone said those three simple words.

Or a time when I wanted it so badly.

And even though I tried not to let myself hope for it, I thought I knew what it would feel like.

Security.

Safety.

Salvation.

Instead, it feels like diving into the ocean myself, knowing I might die as readily as I might find the answers I've been seeking my entire life.

The way she trusted me to tie her up after she's been tied up her entire life and vowed not to bend to anyone again proved it.

I want her like that always.

Not physically, but open with me. Vulnerable. Trusting.

Part of that means being vulnerable with her.

We've spent the past week together, every moment neither of us is working on Stars and I'm not in class and she's not teaching ballet. Last night she stayed over at my place—my father's place—where I cooked her dinner and we watched *Finding*

Nemo, which was actually a pretty good movie once you get behind a fish protagonist.

She's become a seamless part of my life. Part of me.

"Where the hell is it?" the dean blusters as I head up the stairs.

Betty faces him down over the administration desk. "I've been working on it all weekend."

"Unbelievable. This degree of incompetence doesn't happen at other institutions. Trust me. I have colleagues in every state that I'm regularly in touch with, and—"

"Whatever the problem is, it's not to be resolved by reaming out your staff," I cut in.

He storms off to his office and Betty calls after him. "The financials are on your desk for approval..."

I turn to Betty. "You okay?" She nods, but it's unconvincing. "I'm going to slam his head in the door—"

"It's fine, Sawyer. He asked me to work this weekend digitizing some records. He wanted them done for today, but it was my niece's engagement party this week and I skipped out early because I made a cake for her."

What a prick.

"Come on. I need your help."

Betty follows me down the hall and I install her in the guest chair in my office.

"Tea or coffee?"

She frowns. "What are you talking about?"

"It's a serious question."

She leans forward to get out of the chair. "Sawyer…"

"No. You're going to sit and drink a cup of whatever crap I make in the faculty lounge and not do anything else for the next ten minutes."

I go and fix her a drink, adding a donut while I'm at it.

When I return both to her, her eyes brighten. "Oooh. Apple fritter."

I smile and pass them to her, then sit back on the desk, folding my arms.

She takes in the JENGA set on the corner of my desk. "May I?"

Olivia and I have been playing, but I don't mind including Betty.

Betty slides one out from the bottom and sets it on the top. It doesn't move an inch. "There. How was your trip?"

"Dory is in good shape for finals, though the team is losing sleep."

She nods. "I've been looking into more about the

competition. It's a lot of prestige." A look at the door. "Olivia deserves to be on that team."

"She does."

Betty bites into her donut, chewing and swallowing. "I found something in my digitizing this weekend. He's been bringing in more funding than he lets on, and funneling it to places. Expensing his own trips and charging more than they're worth."

"But the department has a lean budget. He's said so at every staff meeting."

"Because he diverts the money to his own interests."

It's one thing for him to be sneaky, another to break rules outright.

Disgust rises up, a bitter taste in my throat.

But on its heels is opportunity.

"Betty," I start, "if the vice provost were to find out, how much trouble would he be in?"

"A lot. But so would the rest of us. There would be a full review and investigation. A lot of things dug up."

The door flies open and the dean stands in the doorway. "Redmond. What the hell is this?" He holds up a sheaf of papers. "You took students away for the weekend and billed part of it to the department?"

"Olivia's donation was intended to support the team."

"It was a sham."

"But the money was real. Unless it was returned to her?"

His gaze narrows. "That budget is spoken for. Betty, give us the room."

"She can stay."

The dean slams down the papers, knocking the JENGA tower onto the floor.

Betty jumps in her seat, her coffee spilling on her clothes and the chair.

I spring toward the bookshelf for tissues, yanking out several and handing them to Betty.

She takes a steadying breath. "What I said about job security? I might have changed my mind. I think I'm ready to go to the vice provost's office. I just need to make a few photocopies first."

***

"That's our evidence," I conclude. "You can't possibly allow him to keep his position given what we've laid out to you."

Betty nods quickly from the other chair opposite the vice provost's desk.

"You don't get to tell me what I do and do not allow, Professor Redmond," the woman replies. She's wearing a suit in a soft purple color, but there's nothing gentle about the expression on her face. "These are serious accusations."

"Yes, there've been a lot of those circulating of late."

She shoots me a quelling look and steeples her fingers on the desk. "Allegations of mismanagement and fraud have a process which needs to be followed. Are there any other claims you'd like to make?"

In the past twenty minutes, she's thumbed through the documents Betty brought, her expression unreadable.

I wish she would be less of a politician and more of a human.

A silver frame in the corner of her blotter holds a photo of her and two teenagers. A son and a daughter, most likely.

"Just a moment." I step into the hall and hit a number on my phone. "It's me. Would you be up for what we discussed?"

I return to the office. "We have one more account to share."

A few minutes later, there's a sharp knock on the door. I rise to open it.

"You don't have to do this," I say by way of a greeting.

"I want to." Madison squares her shoulders and comes in.

I stand back, offering her my chair which she takes.

"The dean has been unprofessional with me. Multiple occasions, but most recently when I was a guest at the faculty social and he asked to show me his upstairs bedrooms."

The vice provost's eyes widen.

"It was super uncomfortable," Madison finishes. "Fortunately, Professor Redmond intervened."

"I see. Well, thank you for sharing your accounts. All of you."

I walk Madison and Betty to the door before turning back.

"You've been saving this up," she sighs.

I shove both hands in my pockets. "He was a liar and a cheat when I was a grad student here. But I didn't know half of what he's doing now."

"Are you quite finished for today? Or shall I double up on my blood pressure pills this afternoon?"

"Nearly finished," I promise, and she folds her arms over her chest. "Olivia's suspension was on two grounds: the keycards which every student uses, and money which we have only his word against hers on how that went down. He threatened to take the competition away from her and her teammates unless she could secure funding from her parents.

She couldn't go to her father, so she found another source. If she was your child, would you punish her for trying to save her future?"

Her lips purse. "I'll review the terms of her expulsion personally."

"I trust you'll make the right decision." I rise from my seat, looking up when she speaks once more.

"One more thing, Professor. It's easy to find fault in leadership. But the cracks often cover up deeper flaws, and they're not always the ones we expect."

"Meaning…"

"This university has a long tradition. And the department has strong roots, but even roots can decay over time. A tree that appears healthy on the outside can be rotted on the inside."

"And you're telling me not to cut into it? I'll take my chances."

22

OLIVIA

I knew my roommate was talented, but I didn't know she was such a genius.

The curtain falls on the play Jules produced, and Kat and I leap to our feet, applauding loudly, our cheering even louder than the rest of the full auditorium.

We tote the huge bouquet of flowers I bought in town this afternoon backstage where the cast is congratulating one another and celebrating with a bottle of champagne.

"That was incredible!" Kat declares. "You are the next Stacey Mindich. Daryl Roth. Jeffrey Seller with tits."

"Flowers are usually for the cast," Jules answers with a smile.

"Tonight, they're for you."

My phone vibrates with an email and I check it.

Miss Barclay,

Your application for readmission has been considered and approved.

It's signed by the provost's office.

Disbelief slams into me.

I reread the email twice more, my breath squeezed between my ribs.

This can't be happening.

I check the attachment, which contains an equally brief but formal letter complete with the university's return address and seal.

It's real.

The backs of my eyes burn.

"You okay?" Kat asks.

I swipe at my cheeks. "Yeah. Happy tears."

She leans over my shoulder, her nails digging into my arm when she reads the email. "About fucking time you're back in!"

"Into what?" Jules demands.

"Liv's back to the student life."

Jules joins the group hug. "That's amazing news!"

"Tonight's your night," I protest. I'm already giddy from my friend's victory and trying to process what this development means.

"It can be both of ours. What's college unless you have your friends to celebrate with you?" Jules holds out her champagne and I take a long sip.

Another cast member runs over to hug Jules, and I duck into a corner with my phone.

I need to tell Sawyer. I need to tell everyone.

Liv: Guess who's a student again?

I send a screenshot of the email to Madison too.

It's halfway through the semester, with the Stars finals less than two weeks away. Can I even get into classes this winter?

The ring comes a moment later.

"Wow, phoning students at night to check up? That's full-service, Professor," I answer breathlessly.

"I'm not calling my student—you're not in my class, or any classes, if you need me to remind you. I'm calling the woman I love."

I grin. Damn it feels good to hear him say that. All of it.

But he doesn't sound surprised by my news. "You did this," I realize.

"Betty helped. And Madison."

"Thank you," I whisper.

"You deserve it. You deserve better than this place. But they're lucky to have you."

My phone jumps in my hand.

"Madison's calling. Can I catch up with you later?"

"Sure. I have to get ready for class."

Pretty soon I'll be saying the same thing.

I hit the transfer button and pick up Madison's call.

"You're back in?!" she demands when I answer.

"I'm in! Team Double V is back. Wait, are you genuinely happy for me?"

"No," she scoffs. "But I'd like to see your ass having ten hours of labs a week like the rest of us instead of teaching toddlers how to pirouette."

"First, that's legitimate work. Second...I'm actually looking forward to labs too."

"How does it feel to be back in class?" Jules asks a week later as we sit around the bar.

"So good. And so busy."

The past week has been slammed with work. I'm catching up on almost two months of material.

I'm taking two classes instead of the full-time course load of five. I told Theresa I would keep up my dance teaching schedule because I made a commitment and I won't let her down.

Still, I'm excited to be a student again. It feels different to walk across the hills, tops covered in crisp snow, posters plastered to bulletin boards advertising clubs and socials now that I'm a legitimate part of the club again.

"What are you guys doing for Valentine's Day?" I ask, taking in the banners up around the bar in pink and red. Even the dartboards have pink cut-out paper hearts in the middle.

"Tess and I are going to a concert. And we all know Kat's going to spend it with one of her vag-splitting creations."

Kat grins. "What can I say? Normal guys don't measure up. Although," she goes on, reaching for her beer, "your man's friend had something extra going on at Velvet."

I toss the dart and miss by a mile, hitting the wall below. "Daniel?"

She shrugs. "I think that was his name. We danced a little. He's hot, in a 'takes himself too seriously' kind of way."

"You'd fix that in no time," Jules comments.

"I bet he's wild underneath. It's always the quiet ones." Kat lifts her eyebrows and I can only shake my head.

He hasn't mentioned a damn thing since the night at Velvet, even though I've seen him at ballet twice.

"What about you?" Jules asks me. "Did Sawyer plan something?"

"He broached the subject, but I put my foot in it before he could finish by telling him Emma and I used to spend V-Day together." I wince. "He said there was no reason to break tradition on his account."

Which was sweet, but also a little disappointing. I've barely seen Sawyer, except in the lab, and I miss him.

"Are you going to?"

"Emma and I have barely spoken." I frown and toss another dart, this one landing in the outer ring. "What if this is just how things are now that I'm back in school and she's living with some guy I've met once?"

I retrieve all three and return to the table, setting them between us.

Kat grabs them before they hit the tabletop with a wink. "Only one way to find out."

"Probation," I echo.

Sawyer nods from the driver's seat of his Mercedes. "The dean is off-duty pending a full investigation. Most department extracurriculars are on hold."

I exhale. "Thank goodness Stars got a pass." I stare out the window, the scenery flying by. "Thanks for driving me," I add.

"My pleasure." Sawyer reaches for my hand, pressing a kiss to my palm as we make our way through traffic and into the city. "Couldn't have you missing out on a tradition."

Warmth spreads through me at his touch, and his gesture.

I messaged Emma and asked her to meet me in our usual spot today, with a few changes.

A ringing sound comes over the handsfree and Sawyer answers. "Hello?"

"Sawyer, it's Tate."

My lips slam closed.

At Russell, Sawyer and I have relaxed a little about our relationship, because I'm not taking his class and technically us being together doesn't violate any rules.

But Tate doesn't know, and given the terms for

them going into business together? The news that Sawyer spends his nights whispering dirty things in my ear probably wouldn't go over well.

"I have a meeting for us. A potential first client with enough cash to keep us at capacity for six months. Maybe a year. He's in the Valley, and we can see him face-to-face the day after your Stars competition."

I try to read Sawyer's face, but fail. For once, he's impassive.

"Sounds good."

"It better. After what you pulled this semester staying at Russell, you owe me."

He clicks off and I try to decide which of the questions spinning around my brain to voice.

"Tate was upset you stayed?" I ask.

One shoulder lifts. "It's not a problem. He figured I was seeing through the commitment I made. In a way, I was." His lips twitch. "I wanted to get you back into school. And I did."

"But you need to pick that up soon or you miss your chance."

"Yeah."

Sawyer's helped at Russell, and not only me. The idea of him leaving is hard for me to grasp personally but it's also a loss for the school.

My chest warms at what he's done for me, but I can't help feeling torn.

I'm in love with Sawyer, but love isn't a guarantee of forever. There's still so much uncertainty about what happens for us after this year, but I can't bring myself to raise it because I don't have the answers and neither does he.

We're nearing Midtown, and I force the dark thoughts from my mind and focus on the anticipation. "Almost there."

"You're cute when you're excited."

"You've never had someone you felt better being around? And when things were bad, it messed you up?"

He turns it over. "One time when we were kids, Daniel's grandparents gave him an iPod for Christmas. He already had one and left the second at my house one day. I was envious—of his family, his carelessness. So I sold it to buy something I wanted. When he found out, he was furious. Eventually he got over it, said he didn't care and to keep it. I don't even remember what I bought with it. What I remember is his silence. It fucked with my head. And Daniel's not even my brother."

"Family isn't blood, Sawyer. They're the people you choose to feel that way about." I turn toward him. "Come with me to see Emma."

Sawyer's hand tightens on the steering wheel, his watch flashing in the light. "There are a lot of things I'm good at. Family relationships isn't one of them. I don't want to fuck up your reunion."

"I want you there," I say firmly, and he turns to meet my gaze. "She matters to me and so do you."

Emotions collide on his face, but finally he nods.

Near Bryant Park, we find a place to leave the car and walk the rest of the way.

It's beautiful and snowy, people skating at the rink.

I wrap my coat around me and spot my sister on skates, stepping out onto the ice.

Next to her is Trey. He's tall and good-looking, a scarf tucked into his leather jacket.

But when he steps onto the ice, he wobbles.

I suck in a breath.

"What is he doing?"

"He's trying to skate. For her."

I tug Sawyer over to the edge of the rink. They're on their second pass by when he falls on his ass.

Emma helps him up, grinning, and he kisses her.

I whistle as loud as I can.

She turns slowly, her mouth curving in a wide smile.

Trey murmurs in her ear and she nods.

Emma skates over to me. "You made it! Both of you."

"This is a tradition. I couldn't miss it."

"Hi. I'm Trey." He takes off a glove and extends a hand.

"This is Sawyer," I say, and they shake.

"This your first time on skates?" I ask Trey and he grins, self-deprecating.

"Nah, I'm still waiting for my agent to call. Gonna sign to one of those pro hockey teams any day now."

Sawyer turns to look toward the booth at one end of the rink.

"Trey. Why don't you give the sprints a rest and we can go get skates for me and Olivia. You can show me some of those moves."

I'm so proud of Sawyer and grateful for him. The guys head off and it's just me and my sister.

"How are you?" I ask Emma as she steps toward the edge of the rink.

"Good. Great, actually." She glides along as I walk next to her.

"Listen." I grab her arm and she spins gracefully to face me. "I didn't mean to judge you about Trey, and I'm sorry if I made you feel like I was. No matter what you want, I'm here for you." I wrap my scarf tighter around my neck, tucking it into my coat.

"I'm sorry I didn't tell you. It happened so fast

and I figured you'd try to talk me out of it."

"I would have. I guess our entire lives I felt like I needed to protect you from our parents, especially Mom. Maybe I had ideas of what your life would be like, too."

"You're acknowledging you agree with Mom."

I wrinkle my nose. "Don't tell her."

She bends to pick up a chunk of snow, patting it into a flat shape between her pink mittens. "It's hard living away from home. I had to do my own laundry for the first time last week. I shrunk a Givenchy sweater so badly it won't even fit Kismet. Plus, the guys aren't used to having a girl around. But I did get back on cheerleading."

I smile. "That's great, Ems. Trey looks like he really loves you."

She bites her lip, glancing over to where the guys are receiving skates from the woman working at the stand. "Same for Sawyer."

"We're in a good spot. Did I tell you he's the one who got me back into Russell?"

"That's pretty major. Why don't you look happier?"

The call with Tate from the car about Sawyer's future comes back.

"I don't know what's happening after this semester. Sawyer's starting a new business with this other guy, and he'll go back to the life he had before he came to Russell."

"Has he said that?"

"No. But this is what he wanted before we even met. I can tell he lived for running his own company. This year was just delaying the inevitable. No matter what he says now, it'll change things. Maybe...maybe what we have will be over."

Her eyes fill with compassion, but before she can respond, the guys return with skates and hot chocolate.

"I didn't know if you wanted marshmallows." Trey frowns. "So I got one with and one without."

Sawyer and I exchange an amused look. Trey's cute, and obviously trying hard for my sister.

Icy cold streaks down my spine and makes me shriek.

"You don't think I forgave you that easily, did you?" she asks, all innocence.

I pull out the back of my jacket, trying to shake the snow out to no avail.

It melts, wet and sticky against my skin, plastering my clothes to my body.

My gaze narrows.

"Boys," I start, "you're going to have to hold on to those for a few minutes."

Then, we fight.

23

OLIVIA

During the flight to California, the nerves start to settle in.

"Wow. Look at the trees," Andy says as he points at palms out the window of the shuttle from LAX.

He and Daniel decided to come since it's Andy's birthday and he's never been to the West Coast.

The competition is tomorrow. Tonight, we get Dory and the tank set up and do our final preparations before presenting to the judges. Our entire year comes down to this.

But it feels bigger than that

We'll win or we'll lose.

But what happens next matters too.

After landing and getting our bags, Royce, Adam, Madison, Sawyer, and I head to the trade show center hosting the finals.

"I'll get the hotel keys," Madison volunteers.

"Great." I look around. "I'll get us checked in. Can you make sure Dory's in the right place?"

"No problem." Royce and Adam head off while I get into the line with Sawyer.

"You ready for this?" The back of his hand brushes my palm, and I wish he could grab my hand right here.

"Yeah. No big deal. Just my entire year on the line." I force a smile. "Are you ready for your meeting with Tate?"

"It's not until after the competition. We have plenty of time."

I scan the huge room, my gaze landing on a familiar figure in a dark suit.

"Then why is Tate heading this way?" I murmur.

"Redmond. There you are." Tate pulls up next to us. "Hi there, Olivia."

I smile and nod. "Hey."

I jerk my hand away from Sawyer's.

"Our meeting got moved up," Tate tells Sawyer, checking his watch. "Our client has to fly to Hong Kong tomorrow, and this is the only chance to meet him for the next month. We need to go."

Sawyer frowns, looking back at me and then the registration table.

As if he wants to stay with me.

"It's fine, Professor," I say pointedly. "We've got this. I'll see you later. In the morning, I mean."

This competition will shape my future, but this meeting could shape his.

The idea of him finishing up at Russell and moving on to the next chapter of his life makes me nauseous.

But since I met Sawyer, he's been devoted to ensuring I get the things I want. I owe it to him to support him every bit as much, and not to let anything—even my own desires—get in the way.

Sawyer looks like he's going to argue, but finally relents and heads off with Tate.

The nerves return, but I collect our packages and badges before heading back to the hotel.

I pull up in the doorway of the room to find Madison unpacking inside.

A couple of months ago, we were doing this same thing at regionals before she caught me with Sawyer.

She looks up from her suitcase. "I picked the bed by the window. Don't pretend it's a problem because you're not planning to sleep in this room anyway." She pulls out a keycard. "Two doors down. This is Redmond's. I figure you can hang onto it."

I leave my bag by the door and go to take the keycard she offers.

"Wanna go smoke?" she asks as she finishes, setting her suitcase in the corner.

My jaw drops. "You didn't bring weed to finals."

"I didn't." But her mouth twitches. "Gah. I feel like I have ants in my stomach. There's no way I'll be able to sleep tonight."

"This time tomorrow it'll be all over one way or another."

I sink onto the bed and grab my necklace and she follows the motion.

"Where's Redmond?"

"Went for a meeting with his future business partner. He wanted to stay with us, but I told him we'd be fine."

"You're worried about him," Madison reads.

"No. I'm focused on the team. A hundred and ten percent," I vow.

"It's okay, Liv. I know I gave you a hard time about him, but I was wrong. You can be strong and still want someone in your life. Especially someone like Professor Redmond. He's a decent guy."

I blink up at her, moved by her words. "What changed your mind?"

She folds her arms. "He helped me at winter social. Got me into the party, had my back when the dean was a scummy asshole."

I sit up on my elbows. "He never told me that."

"Well, he did."

My chest expands. I knew Sawyer was amazing, but this is one more reminder.

"Speaking of decent guys, what about you and Royce?" I ask.

Madison flushes. "He's rooming with Adam."

"You'll have the entire place to yourself. Put on some Dolly Parton. Or whatever gets you in the mood... Just saying."

"Yeah, right. Royce and I—" A pounding on our door has us both looking up.

She crosses to it in a few steps and jerks it open.

Royce is there, eyes wide and hair standing up like he's been pulling on it. Adam's behind him, looking almost as agitated.

"What is it?" I demand, shifting off the bed. "Is Dory okay?"

"We've got a problem."

The guys refused to tell us what the issue was as we followed them down to the main floor where all the teams are getting set up.

"What the hell is..." I trail off as I spot the other robot.

"It's Dory," Adam says.

And he's not wrong.

There's another robot that looks suspiciously fish-like.

"Did they copy us?" Madison demands, indignant.

"Not likely. They're from Texas," Royce points out. "Unless they sent spies to Russell, they came up with the idea independently."

We edge closer, until I can read the posters they're mounting next to their project.

"It's not directed for environmental remediation, but scouting deep-sea drilling," I observe.

"So basically killing the planet," Madison says. "That means ours will look better, right?"

"Money talks," Adam counters. "I didn't make the system," he goes on at my look.

This is bad.

The sinking feeling in my stomach is way worse than the nerves from earlier.

The hall is noisy, with the best teams in the country setting up displays of their year's worth of work to be adjudicated by top entrepreneurs and business moguls.

It's brilliant scholarship students like Royce, ambitious activists like Madison, family legacies like Adam...

And me.

I'm not any of those things.

"When are they getting judged?" My voice is a rasp.

There's a schedule posted on the website, and Royce pulls it up, scrolling through the team names.

"Fifth. Before us."

Aaaand now it's worse.

When the judges see their entry first and ours later, it will look as if we copied them. Even if there's no way of proving that.

"It's going to be okay," Madison decides.

"It is?" Adam asks.

"Yes. We just need a plan." She turns to look at me. Adam and Royce follow suit.

"So..." Both her brows lift, expectant. "What's the plan?"

24

SAWYER

"I bet you're glad to be out of there." The energetic fifty-something man in a sport coat drops into a seat next to me in the hotel meeting room a few blocks from the trade show building.

"It's fascinating to see what the next generation is coming out with. But sometimes, it's nice to get back to the real world." Tate extends a hand and the new guy shakes it. "Dave, this is Sawyer."

I shake his hand, too.

"Good to finally meet you," the man says. "I've admired your work for a long time."

"Really."

He nods vigorously. "We've got some aggressive ambitions, and the venture money to back it up. Why don't I tell you what we have in the works and we can discuss whether you're the right partner?"

I nod. "Let's hear it."

Dave talks us through some plans and I try to focus.

But my gaze is drawn to the window behind him. There's a view of the bay, and from the colors in the sky, the sun is setting.

Since Olivia's text to say she was able to get our packet, I haven't heard anything.

The guys better have Dory in place.

And checked that everything's working after the flight.

And—

Pain shoots up my leg and I straighten to see Tate glaring at me.

"We'll have the capacity to deliver," Tate assures him. "Sawyer?"

I blink. "Yes."

"That's a relief. I'm sorry to hear about your father. I met him once, you know. He was a big academic, but you chose right. The Stars competition is a cute way to get kids excited about engineering, but this is for the big boys."

Six months ago, I'd have agreed.

So why is my mind only half here?

Everything is different now.

What I want. What I care about. Where my priorities lie.

And it's because of *her*.

I shove away from the table. "I need to leave."

Tate's face drains of blood. "Sawyer—"

"You're joking." Dave looks between us. "This is a major deal."

"I understand that. And I don't want to waste your time. But there's somewhere I need to be, and it's not here."

I'm out the door before Tate can shout after me.

25

OLIVIA

It's too late to make a new robot, but what we can do is prove that Dory is nothing like the competition.

Dory can help save the planet, but she's also impressive through her maneuverability, her small size, and her flexibility. We're proud of what we've accomplished, and we want the judges to appreciate it too.

We'll highlight our robot's unique capabilities for the judges tomorrow. Which is tough given we don't have all the information on what the other robot does, but we did our best.

After two hours working with the team to hone our presentation, I told Madison, Royce, and Adam we'd done all we could and we'd meet up in the morning.

Instead of finding a spot to eat with them, I let myself into Sawyer's room and opened my computer to go over our notes, past winners...anything that would help give us an edge.

I don't want to let my team down.

I scan more articles from trade publications about new technology advancements, my eyes aching from staring at the screen.

It's not until a creaking sound has me stirring that I realize I fell asleep on my computer.

I turn in my seat to see Sawyer coming in the door, a CVS bag in one hand.

"Hey," I murmur as I straighten. His simple presence lifts my spirits. "I hope that's not your dinner."

"In a manner of speaking." He lets the door close quietly behind him.

"I thought you were supposed to be in meetings with Tate?"

He crosses to me and sits on the bed facing the desk, setting the bag next to him. "No. That's not where I was supposed to be."

"What do you mean?"

Sawyer shifts forward, bracing his elbows on his knees and shoving his hair back from his face. He steeples his hands in front of him and takes me in.

"I was sitting across from this big prospective

client that Tate recruited. The thing I've been working toward for the last year. But all I could think was that none of it mattered as much as I thought. I wanted to be here—with the team, but mostly, with you."

My mouth falls open. "Don't tell me you bailed on the meeting."

"Bail is a strong word. But I did leave early." His eyes crinkle at the corners.

"But...isn't Tate upset?"

"He'll get over it."

Or he won't.

Damn Sawyer being so impulsive.

"You should've stayed," I insist. "You're crazy to walk away from that meeting."

"Or I was crazy to go in the first place."

He closes the distance between us, tipping my chin up. His warm lips ghost over mine, the heat of his mouth waking up every part of me.

"I never expected a woman who could not only steal my breath but change how I breathe. I love you, Olivia. No matter the choice, I choose you. I will always choose you."

His words are everything I didn't know I needed right now.

I grip his wrists and kiss him back.

I want to spend the entire night like this, letting

him show me how much he cares with his words and his body.

But there are problems that won't go away.

At the sudden stiffness in me, he retreats an inch. "What'd I miss?" he asks, sensing my worry.

I explain what happened with the robot and his lips twitch.

"It's going to be okay. You'll fix it."

How can he be so calm?

"You can't know that," I insist.

"I do know that. Because this situation is nothing compared to how broken I was, and you you fixed me. I was fucked up, and you made me whole. Being with you has made me whole."

I'm speechless, the backs of my eyes burning with emotion.

But the confidence in his voice is contagious, and so is the optimism.

How the hell did I find this man?

He shifts back onto the bed and I climb into his lap and lean my head against his chest. "Madison told me what you did for her at the dean's social," I murmur against his shirt.

"Anyone would have." His fingers thread in my hair, stroking.

"They wouldn't have. You did."

I press my lips to his throat, enjoying the rumbling purr that vibrates beneath my mouth.

"Unless you want me to take you to bed this second," he says, "you need to stop doing that."

"Mmm." I really do want that. I want to shut out the competition and the world and let Sawyer remind me nothing else matters. "What's the alternative?"

"I brought emergency supplies."

My gaze shifts past him to the plastic bag on the bed.

He pulls out bread and peanut butter. Then goes to his suitcase to get the JENGA set and lays it out on the carpet.

"You can't be serious."

If I can't be pinned beneath his beautiful body, I should definitely be on my computer coming up with more ways to save us.

But when I take a step in that direction, he grabs my wrist and tugs me toward the floor.

"Get your ass down here, Miss Barclay."

We drop down and play.

Sawyer makes sandwiches using a takeout knife, and I put music on a portable speaker and set up the game.

We take turns sliding blocks from the bottom and setting them across the top.

"You've been practicing," he says when I execute a particularly smooth move.

I arch a brow. "Been taking risks all semester. I've gotten pretty good at it."

He goes next, and the tower wobbles but doesn't fall.

By the time we've built it up to twice its starting height, I'm getting invested.

"No. No, don't do that. Come on, baby," I breathe as I try to lay the next block on one edge of the gravity-defying structure. "Yes!" I exclaim when it balances.

"Need another sandwich."

"Sawyer—!"

He reaches over and knocks the entire thing to the ground.

I flop onto my back on the carpet, laughing as he curses.

"What's so funny?" he growls.

I laugh harder.

Something tickles me between my breasts and I glance down to see a brick getting shoved in my bra. "Hey!"

"Watch it or the next one goes down your pants."

My laughter doesn't stop and Sawyer shifts over me.

"You're delirious," he decides. "You haven't been sleeping."

I finally take a deep breath and grab the brick out of my bra, tossing it up at him. "Before I danced *Swan Lake*, I was up all night. I didn't sleep a moment. It was going to be the best day of my life or the worst."

"But you figured it out."

"Yes."

"And you'll figure this out, too."

Sawyer's lips brush mine.

When he flips us on the bed, intent on making thinking impossible, I believe him.

26

___

OLIVIA

The next morning, I'm out of bed before my phone alarm goes off.

I shower and dress in the clothes I picked out for the occasion.

"Want me to come with you?" Sawyer asks as we start downstairs.

"No. I'm good. Thank you."

I kiss him in the elevator before the doors slide open and I go to meet the team at our booth.

"You guys, dozens of teams came up with great ideas. Ignore them. They don't matter," I announce once we're gathered around.

"Except they do because it's a competition," Royce points out.

"It's a performance," I correct. "Everyone here wants to see something."

Madison grimaces. "I get stage fright."

"We've got this," I insist. "Besides, if we lose don't you feel like we've learned so much?"

Royce and Adam exchange a look.

"Better idea: let's not lose," Adam says.

Royce nods. "Let's pimp this planet-saving robot."

"Go team Double V!" Madison says.

Excitement electrifies me, my nerves turning into anticipation.

The judges start making their rounds. Unlike regionals, we can watch the other projects be judged.

We watch the other team do their presentation. It's polished and smooth, and after, they show a video of their robot performing tasks.

The panel of judges comes around to our booth. It includes a familiar face.

Aliya, the woman Madison and I presented for, is one of the four engineers holding clipboards.

Showtime.

Dancing *Swan Lake* required concerted coordination across every person on stage, but a lot of it was on me as the principal dancer.

This is different.

Madison starts, then Adam, then Royce. I close.

"Of course, videos are fine. But we'd like to show you Dory in action so you can see with your own eyes what she can do."

With theatrical flair, the guys yank the cover off the tank and lower the robot into it with the help of harnesses to bear the weight.

The crowd is quiet while Adam puts it through some challenges.

After, the judges take turns grilling us.

"What gave you the idea?"

"How robust is this design?"

"If your design is selected as the winner, what would be the estimated production cost?"

Finally, there's a curveball.

"If you were given the opportunity to share first place and the prize money with another team, would you?"

We look at each other. Would we split the prize?

"Can you give us one moment?" I pull my team-mates into a huddle. "What do you think?"

Adam shakes his head. "No compromise. If we're good enough to win, we're good enough."

Royce looks uneasy. "But it's all or nothing."

Madison and I stare each other down.

"I don't know, Liv. What do you think?"

I think about what we've been working toward since the start.

I turn back to the judges.

"Yes, we would. If our prototype is exciting enough for the judges, we believe the possibilities will inspire new collaborators and funders to get on board." I look at Aliya. "Maybe another student will see it and build on it in a few years. Engineering is about possibility, but it's also about responsibility."

The judges make final notes on their clipboards and continue on, without betraying any hint as to what they're thinking.

When they turn away, I sag against the table.

Royce claps me on the back.

"That was good," Madison decides.

"I was sweating."

"We've done all we can."

But as I crane my neck to look around the room, I realize someone's missing.

***

SAWYER

"You look like a creeper." Tate stops between me and where I'm standing between two booths, watching my team present to the judges.

"I was going for 'discreet.' Aren't you judging?"

"Not the final stage. We decided it would be too much of a conflict given I'm recruiting from these schools."

"You ever meet a rule you didn't like?" I shake my head. "You must've been a Boy Scout."

"I got kicked out of Boy Scouts. Learned my lesson young." His laugh is dry, and I feel his humor fall away the next moment. "Dave walked out a few minutes after you did last night."

"I'm sorry. I had a conflict."

"It's her, isn't it? She's the reason you left."

I rip my gaze from the team to take him in.

"I wanted this to work out," Tate continues. "But there was one rule, Redmond. Don't get into any more trouble. No women. No scandals."

"She's not a scandal. She's everything."

Tate stiffens in surprise. "You're not serious."

I scan the room until my attention lands on Olivia. "She's the best thing to ever happen to me. If that's a deal breaker, so be it."

He sighs. "You're in this for the long run."

Olivia gestures to the robot, talking animatedly to the judges. I'm so fucking proud of her.

"Forever."

27

OLIVIA

"I can't wait anymore. I'm going to ask them."

Royce grabs Madison's wrist and drags her back. "You won't make them decide any faster."

"They're almost ready," I insist.

"They've been deliberating for hours," Adam complains. "It can't be that hard. Royce, maybe we should go play a game—"

"NO!" Madison and I shout together.

The hairs on my neck lift and I turn to see Sawyer cutting his way across the room.

"Where have you been?" I demand.

"Staying out of the way."

"I like you in my way."

He grabs my hand and surprised pleasure shoots through me.

Moments later, the judges take the stage at one end of the room and Aliya walks to the mic.

"It was an intense competition this year showcasing the best of undergraduate engineering students."

"Yeah, yeah," Adam mutters, his hand flexing.

"The winning teams are sharing the victory. Teams from UC Berkeley and Russell U."

Madison and I grab each other. "Oh my God."

"Wait. We weren't tied with the other fish one!" Royce notices.

The team is all smiles, even Adam.

But there's one person I want to celebrate with.

I throw my arms around Sawyer.

"Knew you could do it," he grunts in my ear.

"Not without you."

Daniel appears, Andy at his side. The kid looks worried. "Is Dory going into your fish tank, Uncle Sawyer?"

"I don't think so."

Sawyer turns to talk to them and I take a deep breath, scanning the room.

One of the competition administrators flags me down. "Could I get you to sign something on behalf of your team—a confirmation you accept the prize?"

"Yes, of course."

I'm doing exactly that when Aliya comes to find me.

"We were really impressed with what you accomplished. And I heard it wasn't an easy time of it, either. We need more people like you." She passes me a card and my eyes widen. "I want to offer you an internship this summer."

"At your firm? In San Francisco?"

She nods. "Think about it. Give me a call."

***

"You aren't sticking around to network?" a guy on the other winning team says after we finish a toast at the competition.

Royce looks persuaded, but Madison hooks his arm in hers. "Thanks, but we have a dinner reservation."

Outside we catch up with Adam on the steps. He's on a video call, grinning in a way I haven't seen him smile in a long time.

"Yeah, my team just came out." He glances up and motions me over, and I lean over his shoulder.

"Hi, Jean. Hi, David!"

"Hi, honey," Adam's mom gushes. "We're so proud of all of you."

"Thank you."

"I gotta go." Adam clicks off and falls into step with me, a few paces behind Madison and Royce. Ahead of them, Sawyer glances back from where he's talking with Daniel and Andy is doing fish impressions. I smile and he winks before letting Andy entertain him.

"Liv, I'm sorry for everything. Especially the video. Hurting you didn't make me feel any better, and it sure as hell didn't bring you back. But I should've known that."

Adam's apology doesn't undo what he did, but it makes me feel better anyway. "You came through in the end. I'm glad you're here."

"Yeah?"

I nod, and he looks up toward Sawyer, lowering his voice. "I hope he's good to you."

"He is. I hope you find someone that's good to you, too."

"I still can't believe we did it," Madison breathes as we catch up to her.

"Me neither."

My stomach growls, reminding me I haven't eaten in too long. I could go for a burger.

Once we get to the restaurant, there's a private room booked with a massive table.

"Wait, this is too big..." I trail off at Sawyer's grin.

Kat and Jules come out from behind a partition. Plus two adults who look like Madison.

"When we heard you won, we caught the first flight. Literally. I did not expect to be wearing this," Kat says, glancing down at her jeans and top.

I hug them both. "You guys are the best."

Servers come out, and we find seats at the table.

Jules and Kat are across from me, Madison on one side of me, Sawyer on the other. Royce and Adam are on the far side, Daniel at the head of the table with Andy between him and Sawyer.

After we order drinks, Adam holds up his hands. "Someone needs to say a few words."

"Go for it." I smile, folding my arms.

Sawyer rises from his seat, looking around the room. "When I started at Russell, I didn't expect to be part of this. I didn't see the point in supervising a bunch of students, and I didn't think I was cut out to do it. But I was wrong, and I'll be forever grateful for that." He looks at me. "Thank you for giving me a first chance, and a second one. I needed both more than I knew."

My throat tightens at the emotion in his voice. "I couldn't be prouder of what you've all achieved, and I enjoyed every minute of it."

"I bet you did," Royce murmurs, and Madison kicks him.

"Okay but there's one thing I don't understand." Kat leans in. "Didn't you guys win half a million dollars?"

We nod.

"So what are you going to do with that?"

We've talked about it but things change when you actually have something.

"Take the cash and run." Royce has us all turning to look at him. "Don't tell me none of you have thought about it. Even you." He nods at me.

"You're right. I'm back in school but I don't know how I'm going to pay for it." Especially since I'll have to do an extra semester of classes.

"You guys need it more. You can have my share," Adam says.

"That's generous. And there's no way, man," Royce counters.

"If you want to take it," I say slowly, "I completely understand. But I want to make sure this project gets used in the real world." I look to Sawyer. "We could start a company still. Couldn't we?"

He nods. "Capital is expensive. Five hundred grand seems like a lot, but by the time you incorporate, hire staff, set up production, it goes quickly."

"Besides we all have another year before graduation," Madison says, making me think of Aliya's offer again.

I totally admire what she's been able to do as a woman in the industry. And I'd learn so much from her.

"You kids don't have to decide tonight," Madison's mother weighs in.

Relief crosses the faces of my teammates, especially Royce, and we go back to our meals.

"That is a big burger," Sawyer comments when my meal arrives.

I grin. "Back off."

"So good," I murmur after taking the first bite.

"Listen." His hand finds my thigh. "There's something you need to know in case it impacts your decision about what to do with your Stars money. Your tuition is paid for next year. And the year after that."

Confusion has me frowning. "That's impossible. How?"

He turns to face me more fully. "Your mom. She didn't want me to tell you. She had money saved even before everything your father went through."

My chest expands. "She did this for me?"

A nod. "She wanted you to have your dreams. But she didn't want you to feel obligated."

"Why are you telling me now?"

He brushes a piece of hair behind my ear. "Because I'm not in the business of keeping things from you, even when it's for your own good."

I lean in and brush my lips across his. "You're the best."

After dinner finishes, I head outside and pull out my phone and hit a contact.

"Olivia," Mom answers. "Is everything all right?"

As I stare out over the skyline, I clue into the fact that it's late on the East Coast. "Did I wake you?"

"It's fine."

I nod even though she can't see me. "We won. The contest, the entire thing. We actually share first prize, but it's the first time any remediation technology has won."

"I don't know what half of that means but congratulations."

I smile, hard enough my face hurts. "Sawyer told me about the money for tuition."

She's quiet for so long I wonder if she's hung up. "I've been saving for the right thing. I can't think of a better investment than my daughter."

Tears prick the backs of my eyes. "Thank you. Um—" I notice the time on my phone. "I'm sorry if I woke you."

"Don't be. I'm glad you did."

28

SAWYER

"If you haven't studied, I'll know next week. I'm not pulling any punches on this midterm."

My second-year class groans as they pack up for the day.

I want to get out of here, as I'm meeting with the vice provost then I have lunch with Daniel and Olivia.

But a line of students forms in front of me—no doubt wanting intel on the forthcoming exam.

"Professor Redmond," the first student starts, "I heard the Russell team won the Stars competition last week."

"They did."

"Is there an application process for next year's team? I want to be on it."

I blink back at him. "Ahh—"

"I do too," the girl behind him weighs in.

A chorus of voices rises up.

What the actual fuck?

"There will be a democratic way of selecting next year's team. That way has not yet been finalized. Are there questions about the midterm?"

A dozen heads shake.

"These are all about Stars."

Nods follow.

The feeling in my chest is pride, and awe that there's so much interest.

"Go study," I tell them. "If you all crush your midterm, we can talk about Stars."

I grab my phone to check my email before departing for my next meeting.

A throat clearing has me looking up.

"I knew there had to be one question about the midterm..."

Except it's not a student.

"Graham." I surprised him last time. Evidently, he's returning the favor.

My former business partner straightens his suit. "It's strange seeing you in front of a class."

"Not as strange as it is seeing you in my class."

There's no reason for him to be here, unless perhaps they're doing a recruiting event on campus.

"It's nice of you to stop by but you should return to whatever purpose brought you here." I check my watch. "I have a meeting in—"

"I came to see you." His jaw works, brows pinched as if he's chewing glass. "Christine told me the truth. Evidently, she wanted to help Dwayne get promoted, and he convinced her the only way to do it was to get you out of the way. He manipulated her, spreading lies about you and offering her money and connections if she went along with his plan to accuse you."

His words stun me silent.

When I finally speak, my voice is cautious. "How did this come out?"

"She said she met one of your students. That meeting made her realize she needed to confess the truth."

Olivia.

Every good thing that's happened, she had a hand in.

"I'm so fucking ashamed." Graham exhales heavily.

"Don't blame your daughter." My voice is sharp. "She's young and was caught up. Dwayne took advantage of her."

She shouldn't have lied—not even for my sake, but because women deserve to be believed.

Still, it was brave of her to admit what happened after the fact and face the consequences.

"I blame myself for not seeing what was going on." He shoves both hands in his pockets.

"And that's why you came here. To tell me this."

"No. I came to tell you that I fired Dwayne. I want you to come back to the company."

It's a staggering offer from the man who only wanted me gone a year ago.

I reach for my bag on the table near the lectern, my hand gripping the handle tight.

"Already cashed out. Financially and mentally." I shake my head, starting for the door.

He grabs my jacket. "I get it, Sawyer. But we're not the same without you. I'll make it worth your while. Whatever you want. Risky projects. Restructuring the company. As long as we take care of our employees, you can have fifty-one percent. The final say in all decisions."

Hearing the words I imagined him saying, all of them saying...

It's what I've been wanting for years.

The chance to take more risks, to do work the accountants didn't immediately agree to. To focus more on innovation and less on cash.

I could be redeemed in the eyes of my former employees.

Exonerated, for all of it. I would have the vindication I've craved for so long.

"I'll think about it."

He shakes his head in disbelief. "You're not understanding what I'm saying. I'm offering you everything you wanted, everything we argued over—"

"I understand perfectly."

He wants to give me my life back, or the part he can grant me.

New York and my old employees and the business I worked to build.

An apology from the people who turned their backs at the first sign of trouble.

When I first came to Russell in the fall, this was all I dreamed of.

"But what would you do instead? You're not going to stay here forever." He gestures around the classroom. "This place is your past. Distant history."

"Why don't you spend more time worrying about your own business. Let me worry about mine."

I stop in at my office to get some Stars paperwork on the way to my meeting with the vice provost.

There's a stack of papers on my desk, and when I move them, a small piece of plastic falls out.

My dad's department credit card.

Not using that for a while given the investigation the department is under.

I turn to stick it back in the drawer of the Go set, but the drawer is stuck. It takes me a moment to work it open, because there's an item caught inside.

A small leather journal, barely larger than my palm.

My phone dings with an alarm, a reminder that my meeting starts in ten minutes.

Instead of heading for the door, I hit the snooze button and open the cover of the book.

My father always kept logs of his work. This one starts a few months before I left.

Records of experiments, projects he was trying, and ideas for class fill the blank sheets, the date written crisply in pencil in the top right corner of each.

But about a quarter of the way in, the entries change. I flip through the pages, bittersweet memories rising up.

The dates are still there, but instead of numbers and sketches, the pencil marks flow into sentences and paragraphs.

He left this week. Walked out in the middle of the night and didn't come back.

I suppose we had an argument. But it wasn't even that. He stood accused of cheating and instead of pleading his case like a reasonable human, he told me once it wasn't true. Then when I pressed him, asking if he had evidence, he stared through me then turned on his heel and went upstairs.

I'm waiting for him to appear at the door or on campus. I'd even take one of those withering looks he perfected as a teenager.

They're about me, I realize.

Every thought. Every note. Every regret.

His reflections on our interactions, ones I didn't realize he gave a second thought to beyond dismissing me as incorrigible, run together in an endless stream of consciousness.

I keep reading, flipping page after page.

I keep thinking about the night he left. What I should have said.

It's not that I didn't believe him, but truth leaves behind proof.

Doesn't it?

What if I should have ignored proof for once and focused on trust?

I was resentful this fall after finding my father's

letter to Olivia last semester, as if it meant that he cared for her in a way I never experienced while living under his roof.

But he kept an entire journal of stories about me.

My throat works, my muscles tightening as I remind myself to breathe.

In.

Out.

The self-assured man questioned himself. Not aloud, not in public, but in private. In his head, the most sacred venue for a man who made his living with ideas, he doubted. He struggled.

He wanted things to be different.

He never told me.

If he had...

Maybe we could have sorted things out before it was too late.

I shut the cover of the journal and stare at the cover.

So what? It is too late.

Except...

I think back to Graham's visit. The events of the past ten months.

We don't always do our best work when we're called to do it. But we can learn and forgive and never stop trying.

Even when it doesn't look like it, other people might be trying, too.

My phone alarm sounds again, the snooze having expired. The meeting starts in one minute.

I tuck the journal in my jacket before heading out.

29

OLIVIA

"Okay, Andy, now keep turning to the left. Other left. There you go."

"Miss O, when do we get to see the costumes for the recital?"

"Ahh, it's only March."

"I want to be a fish. No, a whale."

"The theme is supposed to be flowers," one of the girls points out, and Andy frowns.

"Maybe there's room to compromise," I murmur to him under my breath. He breaks into a wide grin and I cut a look at Theresa, watching from the other side of the glass.

I'm teaching guppies and loving it. Not only do I get to dance, but I get to see others discover the same love.

Once the class lets out, I shepherd them toward the door.

"They adore you," Theresa murmurs.

"I love them."

She nods to a small fabric bag in the corner of the studio near the stereo system. "That hasn't moved in weeks."

"Yeah, I've been using the studio a lot at night. I hope that's still all right."

"I'm thrilled for you. I actually want to talk to you about the summer. We've always run dance camps, and I'd love it if you would consider teaching. Depending on your plans and whether you're taking classes."

"I don't have plans yet," I admit. "I might take a class virtually, but not a full course load."

"Well, think about it."

My phone buzzes with a text.

Sawyer: We need to talk. I'll pick you up after dance class.

The happiness at seeing his name—which I changed back from Repentant Asshole because given our relationship it seemed right to put us on even ground—

is tempered by the black and white words on the screen.

"Everything all right?" Theresa asks.

I flash a smile. "Great."

I text back.

Liv: It's fine, I'll meet you at your place.

"Hey. Can I get a ride with you?" I ask Daniel when he comes in to collect his son.

"Sure thing," he says as he starts bundling Andy into his winter clothing, a process that inevitably takes a few minutes.

I run upstairs to change into street clothes and return when Andy is pulling on his boots.

We pile into Daniel's truck, Daniel fastening Andy into the car seat.

"I just realized I've never been in your truck before."

"And that's weird why?"

"I feel like I know you. Between dance, and you coming to California for Stars..."

"Your friends jumped on a plane and were there in half a day. That was impressive."

"That's Kat for you. Following the YOLO tattoo on her ass."

"What's ass?" Andy demands, and I cringe. I forgot he was in earshot.

"Vegetable," Daniel answers smoothly. "Really green. Lots of leaves."

Andy makes a disgusted face and turns back out the window.

I bite my cheek against the laughter.

"Does she?"

"Hmm?" I glance back at Daniel to see his hands gripping the steering wheel.

"Have a tattoo?"

"Not anywhere visible. You'll have to ask her."

He's quiet the rest of the way back.

I thank him for the ride and jump out of the truck, crossing the street to Sawyer's place.

I take the path up to the new porch, ascending the stairs. At the door, I ring the bell.

The chimes surprise and delight me.

When the door sweeps wide, I grin.

"You put in a new one. The doorbell actually works."

"Figured I should put the finishing touches on this place. It was getting down to my last chance." Sawyer's eyes crinkle. "Come on in."

I hang my purse and jacket by the door and follow him inside.

There's music in the background.

"Wine?"

"Sure."

He goes to the kitchen and I pad into the living room.

The fish in the tank swim around, beautiful and unaffected. I lean close to the glass, studying their movements.

"Almost as elegant as Dory," Sawyer says from behind me.

He holds two glasses of red wine, and passes me one. "Almost. What's the occasion?"

"You finally getting what my father wanted for you."

"Stars?"

"I meant the fish."

Sawyer reaches under the tank and peels off the tape, holding it up.

He's asking me to take them back.

"Thank you." I lift the piece of tape off his finger, Lancaster's familiar handwriting making my chest ache. "I don't have room for them at Theresa's."

"I thought you might say that."

He sets his glass on the coffee table and paces toward the window. "This whole year started off terrible, with getting evicted from my own company, then Lancaster dying, and coming back here."

I cross to stop behind him, the wood creaking beneath my feet. "It's been a lot."

"You changed all of it."

He turns, rubbing his thumb down my jaw. "Every second with you this year, I felt like maybe all the terrible shit wasn't so terrible. Or if it was…I went through it for a reason. It's all worth it. I'd do it again, every moment"—his gaze falls to his watch—"if it meant being with you."

My heart melts. "I feel the same way."

Sawyer takes a slow breath, his dark, familiar gaze looking straight into my soul. "I need to tell you what happened today."

"Okay." I take a sip of wine to steady my nerves.

"Graham showed up in my classroom." I blink in disbelief. "Christine recanted, explained everything to him. It was because of you. She wouldn't have done it if you hadn't talked to her."

He threads his hand through mine. I don't know where he's going with this, but I'm excited and dreading it all at once.

"He not only offered me my role back, but control of the company. I'd go back to New York. Have more influence and responsibility. Grow the staff and make all the calls."

That's why he finished working on the house. The doorbell was one more finishing touch.

"That's great, Sawyer. Assuming that's what you want," I go on, uneasy.

"It's not. I told the vice provost I wanted to stay and teach."

The words. I know what they mean, but I'm struggling to process anyway.

"Graham said this place was distant history, but he was wrong," Sawyer continues. "History isn't defined in years. It's what shapes you. The company I founded with him? That's distant history, Olivia. This place has opportunities, for me and for us."

There's no oxygen in the room.

I don't need any.

"You're staying at Russell. To teach."

"Mm-hmm. The vice provost agreed on one condition—that I help out with the department. The dean has been fired, which will be public tomorrow, and the administration is a mess. I can help connect companies to the university so there's money and partnerships for engineering. Tate knows about you and me, and at first he didn't understand but he's agreed he can start the company and I'll be a consulting partner. Part-time, because I'll be living here in Elmwood."

"So you're staying," I say again, feeling stupid.

His expression is full of warmth and love. "That's the plan. What do you think?"

I start to drop the glass, and he saves it.

"Think I need to sit down," I whisper.

He crosses to the couch and sinks onto it, pulling me into his lap so I'm straddling him. He sets my glass on the table and tugs my hips against his.

"You're the best thing that's ever happened to me. I love you, Olivia. All your perfection, all your imperfections. I want to live in awe of you forever."

I can't breathe. Can't even think. "I don't know what to say."

"Say yes. I want you to move in here. Nothing against Theresa, but I've had enough climbing fire escapes. Please say yes."

I'm too choked up to speak.

I carefully peel the tape off my fingers and press it to his shirt.

For Olivia Barclay.

I like seeing my name on him.

"So to be clear, I get the fish and you?"

He grabs my face and pulls me down to him, kissing me fiercely.

I wrap my arms around his neck, glorying in the feel of him under me, his proximity, his scent.

I can stay here with him. All next year, we'll be together. All summer—

Shit.

My mouth wrenches away from his, and he has the decency to look offended.

"This summer. Aliya offered me an internship in San Francisco."

I should turn it down. It's only fair given he made a decision for me, for us, and this would mean I'm leaving him again.

"Well that's too bad. You're going to have to make it up to me with lots of phone sex."

My brows lift. "You mean it? You don't mind?"

"It's a great opportunity. Better than anything here. And I heard your last supervisor was an asshole."

I laugh, shifting to get more comfortable over his thighs and feeling him harden as a reward for my efforts. "She offered to pay me a really good salary. Enough that I could afford to pay my own tuition next semester, plus I can fly back to visit."

"Don't worry, sweetheart. I'll come to you."

I bite my lip. "You better."

"When would you leave?"

"May."

"That's only two months away. In that case, we need to spend every second together in the meantime."

He carries me up the stairs.

EPILOGUE

SAWYER

August

"Think we have enough drinks?" I survey the kitchen with a critical eye.

"I'm sure she didn't turn into an alcoholic in San Francisco," Daniel comments.

"It's possible." Zander shrugs helpfully.

I shoot my friends a glare. "I meant for the crowd."

"Did someone say drinks?" Ric and his wife appear in the front door, him toting a case of beer and her with a full-looking bag with the label from a fancy wine store in town.

"Good. Thanks." I take the wine from Ric's wife, relief washing over me.

I hope Olivia likes it.

Not only the party, all of it. I've been working on the house and I have news for her.

The noise of tires outside has me dropping the beer I'm holding and heading for the door.

"You can't bail on this," Zander calls.

"I heard a car."

"Wow, are you a dog now?" Daniel demands.

Of course, I wanted to be the one to pick Olivia up at the airport. But she flew into JFK and her parents asked to pick her up. They're working things out, and she invited them to come to the BBQ today.

Now, I jerk open the front door to see the car on the street.

Olivia's mother gets out of the front, her father standing behind the open trunk.

The back door moves, and Emma shifts out.

She waves to me and I wave back, but I'm tense. She's not who I'm looking for.

"Dad, I've got it."

Olivia's voice comes from behind the lid of the trunk, and as they shut it, she appears.

My heart stops.

I saw her three weeks ago, but it feels like three years.

She's fucking stunning. In skin-tight jeans and a black off-the-shoulder top, sunglasses perched on her head. Her dark hair swings in a curtain that brushes her collarbone.

"Hi."

Somehow my feet carry me across the porch toward the driveway.

She looks up, her gaze meeting mine, and her lips curve. "Hi."

The electricity crackles to life between us.

"Olivia," her father says, "we could leave this bag in the trunk and drop you at your place after."

"No," we say at once.

"But your dorm room—"

"I won't be going there for a while."

"Leave it be, Dad," Emma calls.

All I see is Olivia. Her full lips shiny, her eyes bright and eager.

She's the same, and different. There's an easy confidence about her that's sexy as fuck.

I step close and thread my hands in her hair, needing to know she's really here.

"Hi," I say again, because words are hard and overrated anyway.

When I pull her mouth up to mine, she meets me halfway.

Every time I've imagined kissing her, it's never been like this.

She's here and mine and open and wanting and unafraid.

"You must be Olivia's family." Daniel's pointed voice from the porch pulls me back.

"It's good to see you," Olivia murmurs. "And I like your path."

She nods to the river rock walkway I made this summer.

"Had some stones lying around."

It's a joke, but I did sprinkle the ones from my collection as a kid in amongst the landscaping rock.

There's no point carrying them around with me. I don't need to search for home.

I've found one.

My dad would have been happy to see this.

The thought comes out of nowhere, but I know it's true.

He didn't understand how to connect with me. But he tried. And later, he figured it out, with Olivia and his other students.

He would have liked to know I made it back here. That after all we've been through, we're better than before.

Olivia's eyes warm, and I wonder if she knows what I'm thinking. She sees so damn much. It's one of the million reasons I'm crazy about her.

"Why did we decide to have a BBQ?" I whisper.

That means hours before we'll be alone.

"To catch up with everyone we love after the summer and before classes start."

My head is shaking before she finishes. "I love no one."

She laughs and grabs my hand, tugging me up the walkway following her dad with her suitcase.

OLIVIA

Halfway through the party, I couldn't be happier to be back.

My parents and Emma and Trey are having a good time. Trey is introducing my dad to a new kind of beer.

Andy and one of his friends, a boy with a difficult home situation that Sawyer has been spending time with through a social services group, are practicing their dance moves in the sprinkler.

Sawyer's friends are playing with water balloons

in the backyard, and after she and Jules and I swap summer stories, Kat offers to take them on.

I spend not nearly enough time next to Sawyer. But the closer I get to him, the more torturous it is not to be alone with him.

Was he always this hot?

He's even hotter in a dark shirt and jeans, his hair pulled back, his grin easy and generous as he drinks a beer with everyone we care about. It's the opposite of the department BBQ he hosted here eight months ago.

Since then so much has changed.

I got kicked out and readmitted. We won Stars and gave half the money to the non-profit to work on a prototype to help with environmental remediation. My parents downsized and wound up in couples counseling and my dad is getting help for his problems. My sister and Trey are incredibly solid, and not only did she finish exams with high marks but he looks at her like she makes the sun come up every morning.

And as for me and Sawyer...

We're stronger than ever.

We talk every day, and he's so much more open about everything: where his head is at, what he wants in life, how his past has shaped him for better and worse.

We laugh. We laugh so damn much.

And I'm more in love with him than I knew was possible. He treats me like gold—not something sacred and fragile, but something to be appreciated and enjoyed.

"I'm impressed you've kept them alive all summer," I comment as I pause in front of the fish tank on a trip inside to top up drinks for my parents.

Sawyer comes to stand behind me, wrapping an arm around my waist and pulling me back against him. "Captain Jack is thriving."

"Since you're such an animal whisperer..." I pause. "My parents are going on a cruise together. Their first solo vacation in years. They're wondering if we can take Kismet."

"I'm sure we can take care of a dog. It's like a fish right? Feed it flakes. Clean its water."

I turn in his arms and kiss his smartass mouth. "We'll figure it out," I murmur against his lips.

After dinner, we start a bonfire. The guys were thoughtful enough to set out chairs and wood stumps to sit on. When it gets dark, I realize the fenced yard is surrounded by fairy lights.

"What's holding them up?" Emma asks and I grin.

"Cutlery. From Fall Ball. Sawyer was mad at his dad, so he glued them to the fence."

"That's a good one," Trey decides. "I should do that to one of my brothers' cars."

"Excuse me," Sawyer says, raising his voice so everyone turns to look. "Now is the time for the special event."

"What special event?"

"My good friend is performing."

Daniel's brows shoot up. "I am?"

"Yeah. That's why you brought the guitar."

"That's why you asked me to," he realizes.

I'm tugged behind the corner of the house.

"What's going on?"

"He's a distraction. Can't wait any longer."

I suck in a delighted breath but can't resist teasing him.

"Wait, it was your idea to have an end of summer party."

"Mm-hmm. And now we're going to have our own party."

"You mean you want to hear about the internship? Or the little sushi place I found the second to last week I was there?"

He tugs me up the stairs. "That can wait."

"What can't?" I ask, innocent, as he drags me down the hall.

In the master bedroom, my heart stops.

"Sawyer, it's beautiful."

It's painted a soft color, everything redone.

"I know we decided you'd keep a place on campus with Kat and Jules for when you need your own space, but I want you to feel at home here too. I figured you could put your dance stuff here." He points to a dresser with lots of little drawers and a huge mirror. "Daniel helped me work on it."

"It's incredible." I run my fingers over it, but stop when I notice what's sitting on top.

The shell lamp I brought back from the flea market in New York.

It's such a small thing, but having it here reminds me of how he accepts me. All of me. No matter what.

"You're incredible."

He looks at me over my shoulder in the mirror with complete and utter devotion.

Then moves closer, pinning my hips against the wood with his. His mouth curves wickedly.

"Missed this."

"My ass?"

"Not only your ass." His hands skim up my sides, cupping my breasts, and I could purr.

"Also my boobs."

"Exactly."

But his touch is so distracting, I can't complain. I arch back against his hard body, trailing my hand around his neck.

The sound of the guitar and a voice singing over top drifts in the open window, dragging my attention from the irresistible man in front of me.

"Wow. Daniel's really good. We're missing out."

"I've been missing out. Spending the summer apart nearly killed me."

"How long do you think we have?" I murmur, my gaze drifting to the little dormer window at the end of the room, the stars and light from the bonfire visible through it.

"Not long enough."

His lips on my neck are a whisper of perfection.

He turns and hitches my legs around his waist. I tighten my grip on him and he hisses out a breath.

"Have you been working out, Cherry?"

"Found a place to dance while I was in California," I whisper against his mouth. "I'm bendy, too."

"Fuck, I'm going to take you for hours." He reaches for his belt and in moments, his pants are gone.

I work on my clothes, stripping them off in record time.

His mouth bends to suck my nipple through my shirt, the hot wetness delicious enough to make me twist and writhe.

Yes. This is what it should be like.

Sawyer's at my entrance, and the next second, he's using my wetness to sink all the way into me.

"Missed this, sweetheart. Every inch of me missed this."

He pulls out only to rock back into me, enjoying each millisecond of my body's reaction to him.

He's huge and insistent, and we're like a well-rehearsed production that's somehow still new every time.

My nails dig into his neck.

"You keep at that, anyone who didn't know is gonna when we go back downstairs." But he grins, satisfaction and need clashing on his handsome face.

"They'll know you're mine."

His strokes are deep and claiming, and I want to be claimed by him.

I'm his and it's everything.

My breath gets shallow, and so do his strokes as he pistons his hips. His noises say he's getting closer, and damn if I'm not going to fly off soon.

"Oh my God." I clench around him, pleasure ripping through me.

My reaction sets him off, his hips thrusting twice more before his body goes tight. We collapse over the dresser, him still shaking inside me and over me.

My eyes blink open after forever, settling on a photo tucked into the mirror of me with my friends.

And one taken at the Stars finals with the team and my friends and Sawyer.

I grin, still breathless. "Ready for a new year?"

"You mean more of us? I'm so ready."

Thank you for reading *Claim*! I hope you loved Sawyer and Olivia.

Are you longing to experience Sawyer's best friend fighting for his own HEA?

Don't miss Daniel's sexy, swoony single dad romance in *Tempt*...

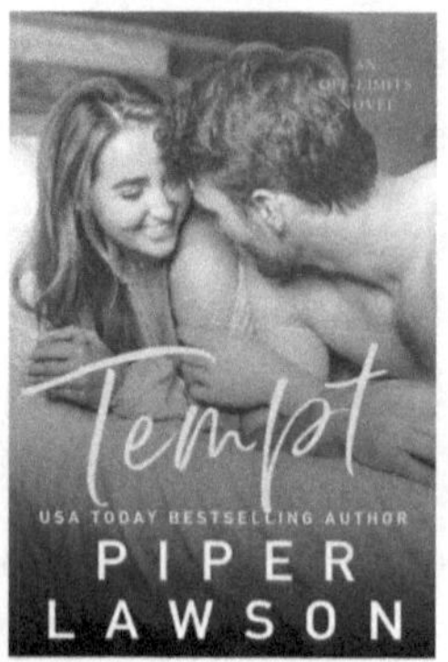

He's a single dad and my new boss.

He's scorching hot, with gorgeous dark eyes and a smile that makes me burn up every time he looks at me. Too bad he's ten years older, with trust issues and more layers than my psych degree could ever unwrap.

I shouldn't fall into bed with him, not to mention let my heart get involved. But he makes me feel things I never expected to feel...

She's my son's nanny, and a student at the university where I'm a professor.

Seeing her play with my kid, hearing her laugh from the bedroom across the hall, watching her walk by with those legs that would look amazing over my shoulders? It's the best kind of torment.

I need to stay professional...but she's too tempting.

Read a short excerpt below

CHAPTER ONE
Kat

Nothing makes a woman feel sexy like dressing up as a stranger.

It could be the tailored white button-down shirt that skims my body.

Or the heeled Mary Janes that click on the sidewalk.

Nope, I decide as I pass a store window and do a quick once-over. *It's the glasses.*

Making my new professors think I'm a serious student the first week of senior year will buy me half a letter grade come finals.

Naturally, I parked myself in the front row of every class today with my best "oh please God, keep talking about that course outline" expression.

Before I can congratulate myself further, a dark, fluffy ball darts between my legs.

The bakery box in my hands slips. It and its precious cargo tumble to the concrete.

I drop to my knees and peek inside the lid.

The contents are intact.

Thank fuck.

From this level, I spot my attacker: the tiniest rabbit ever is huddled against the planter, shielded by the leaves.

"Hey, little guy. Aren't you handsome?"

"Shit!" A short woman runs out of the building nearby, scanning the bushes in the planters lining the street.

"He's with you?"

"Yes." She sighs when she sees him, kneeling down. "His name is Angel. But we might have to change it to Houdini with how much trouble he gets into. He escapes at least twice a week."

The sign for the animal shelter registers in the corner of my eye.

"Hey, Angel," I croon. He perks up, sniffing delicately. "I get it. You're not a sweet Angel. You're a badass Angel, but misunderstood. Like Criss Angel. Or Angel from Buffy the Vampire Slayer."

He tenses, but lets me scoop him up.

"Usually, he won't let us hold him," the woman says, impressed. "He likes you."

"I'm good with boys. Just a matter of understanding what they want." I scratch the bunny's fluffy ear and he leans into my hand, snuggling as if it's his mission in life. "I might bring a guy home, but I never keep him. You know what Angel? You might be my exception."

She reaches into a folder under one arm and produces a sheet of paper. "Adoption application. Just in case."

"Bye, handsome." I give my future best guy one last ear scratch before handing him to the other woman.

I tuck the application into my bag, pick up my box and carry on across the street.

Elmwood has Big Fall Energy. The leaves are teasing they're about to turn gold and red. While the days are still hot, everyone cups their coffee to warm their hands on brisk mornings.

My final year at Russell U will be a victory lap. Graduation's a given, but what really matters is having the time of my life with my roommates and best friends.

I wouldn't have survived without them, and tonight, we're celebrating.

The dance academy occupies an old house, renovated top to bottom. I wind my way through half a dozen dance moms in the hallway to reach the first-floor studio.

Inside, Liv holds court, her dark hair twisted up into a bun on her head and her black bodysuit skimming curves that ended her dream of becoming a professional dancer. Now, she's one of the top engineering students at Russell U—and queen amongst the cute eight-year-olds she teaches ballet to in the evenings.

"See you all next week!" she choruses, and the children start for the door in a tiny mob.

"Hey!" Liv embraces me at the studio doorway. "Cute glasses. This a new prescription?"

I push them up my nose. "You know it's first week of classes. Which means—"

"First impressions," she says at the same time I do.

Since we came to Russell and ran into one another on one fateful night freshman year, Jules, Liv and I have been bonded.

Now, it's our final year of rooming together. Our final year to enjoy the campus, the parties, the friends, even the classes. Basically, all the things we've taken for granted since we arrived as wide-eyed teens.

The one wrinkle is that Liv just moved in with her boyfriend. She comes by all the time, but I'm still working out how to convince her it was a big mistake.

"What's that?" Liv nods to the box.

"A surprise. But first, I have news. A new room-mate. Better than you or Jules." I reach for the adoption application in my bag.

Liv grabs my arm before I can get it. "Really? That's great. Jules thought you might be upset about her leaving."

The air evaporates from the room. "What?"

"Jules is moving in with Tess."

I've been hit in the side of the head. The floor tilts under my feet.

"You didn't know." Liv covers her mouth with a hand. "Shit."

I tug at the neckline of my shirt, popping open another button. "But...They've broken up twice already this year."

Ditching the best roommates you've ever had for some epic romance, like Liv did, is hard enough to take. Nothing against Jules' girl, but their relationship is off-again as frequently as on-again.

"You'll get new roommates," she says, twisting the knife in my stomach deeper.

I think of the horror stories from Jules first year before we decided to room together—her first roommate didn't shower or do dishes.

"Never. I'm like a penguin. I roommate for life." I toss my hair. "Seriously, it's fine. I'll keep the entire place for myself. Kat's Den of Debauchery. Greek Row's only a couple of blocks. Just wait, I'll have an entire frat house worth of juniors tripping over themselves to fulfill my every desire."

Except a big, empty apartment on campus sounds less fun than I'm making it out to be.

Liv squeezes my arm. "Are the three of us still going for Hoes over Brews?"

Are we? I want to ask.

We started the tradition of girls nights at our favorite pub back when we were single. But apparently everyone's paired up.

"Ah—rain check. Classes were more intense than I thought."

Her pretty face falls. "I'm sorry, Kat. I screwed this up."

"You didn't. We'll catch up soon." I let her hug me, but I suddenly feel out of place.

More out of place than I already did being one of the lone tall people surrounded by swarming children.

I turn toward the door, hurried and unseeing, and promptly run into a hard male chest.

The box tumbles toward the ground for a second time today.

This time, my glasses join them.

"Dammit!"

"Excuse me," the chest says.

"How did you not see...?"

I trail off and look up into bottomless brown eyes.

They're accompanied by a gorgeous face and square jaw topping off a hard, lean, and familiar body dressed to East Coast casual perfection in a button-down and jeans. He smells like a sexy forest and from the way his shirt clings, his abs are an eleven out of ten.

"Daniel," I blurt.

"Kat. Hey."

His voice is as beautiful as the rest of him.

"I'm here to get Andy."

"Good. Because taking someone else's child is a felony. You're crushing this single dad thing."

He rubs a hand over his face, hiding a self-deprecating smile.

A professor who's closer to thirty than twenty, Daniel's mature in a way no cocky college boy could compete with.

He's also too tight-laced for his own good.

I'm go-with-the-flow, he's by-the-book.

I'm free spirited, he's responsible.

I'm independent, he has a cute kid who's his whole world since his wife died.

It would never work.

Even if one night, I thought it might.

He bends and retrieves my glasses, and the dance moms watch him without shame. I arch a brow in their direction and they turn back to their conversations.

Daniel holds up the crooked frames. "Sorry about these. I'll replace them."

"Don't sweat it." I slide them up my nose. "They're not prescription. I wanted to look smart." I gesture to the rest of my ensemble and he takes his time soaking it in.

"You're smart already."

He straightens the glasses on my face, his

fingers brushing my cheek so gently I shouldn't notice.

I do notice.

Apparently, it's been too long since I had a physical connection with another person, because the jolt of anticipation has my breath catching.

For a second, I'm no better than the lusty dance moms, except they're across the room and I'm inches away from the hottest guy in Elmwood.

He retrieves the box, turning it right-side up and holding it out.

I peek under the lid. The cupcakes are smooshed, the ones with Liv and Jules' names a clownish smear of icing.

Motherfucker.

"Can I at least give you a ride?"

Daniel's smooth voice brings me back.

"No thanks. I'm flying solo tonight." And a lot of nights, it looks like.

"Sure. It was good to see you."

Buried memories come back in an instant.

His lips at my ear.

His dark eyes trained on me.

The pull between us, the feel of the club music...

The moms are still staring. Evidently Daniel's status as a widower also makes him top of the most eligible bachelor list.

"Get a little closer," I suggest on my way past. "Maybe you can smell him."

But I can't really blame them.

He smells fucking incredible.

End of Sample

To continue reading, be sure to pick up *Tempt* at your favorite retailer.

BOOKS BY PIPER LAWSON

KING OF THE COURT SERIES

After being dumped and losing my job the same week, the last thing my broken heart needs is a rebound.

A steamy, grumpy sunshine sports romance featuring a woman down on her luck, a star basketball player with a filthy mouth, and a connection neither of them can deny.

OFF-LIMITS SERIES

Turns out the beautiful man from the club is my new professor... But he wasn't when he kissed me.

Off-Limits is a forbidden age gap college romance series. Find out what happens when the beautiful man from the club is Olivia's hot new professor.

WICKED SERIES

Rockstars don't chase college students. But Jax Jamieson never followed the rules.

Wicked is a new adult rock star series full of nerdy girls, hot rock stars, pet skunks, and ensemble casts you'll want to be friends with forever.

RIVALS SERIES

At seventeen, I offered Tyler Adams my home, my life, my heart. He stole them all.

Rivals is an angsty new adult series. Fans of forbidden romance, enemies to lovers, friends to lovers, and rock star romance will love these books.

ENEMIES SERIES

I sold my soul to a man I hate. Now, he owns me.

Enemies is an enthralling, explosive romance about an American DJ and a British billionaire. If you like wealthy, royal alpha males, enemies to lovers, travel or sexy romance, this series is for you!

TRAVESTY SERIES

My best friend's brother grew up. Hot.

Travesty is a steamy romance series following best friends who start a fashion label from NYC to LA. It contains best friends brother, second chances, enemies to lovers, opposites attract and friends to lovers stories. If you like sexy, sassy romances, you'll love this series.

PLAY SERIES

I know what I want. It's not Max Donovan. To hell with his money, his gaming empire, and his joystick.

Play is an addictive series of standalone romances with slow burn tension, delicious banter, office romance and unforgettable characters. If you like smart, quirky, steamy enemies-to-lovers, contemporary romance, you'll love Play.

MODERN ROMANCE SERIES

When your rich, handsome best friend asks you to be his fake girlfriend? Say no.

Modern Romance is a smart, sexy series of contemporary romances following a set of female friends running a relationship marketing company in NYC. If you enjoy hot guys who treat their families like gold, fun antics, dirty talk, real characters, steamy scenes, badass heroines and smart banter, you'll love the Modern Romance series.

ABOUT THE AUTHOR

Piper Lawson is a WSJ and USA Today bestselling author of smart and steamy romance.

She writes women who follow their dreams, best friends who know your dirty secrets and love you anyway, and complex heroes you'll fall hard for.

Piper lives in Canada with her tall and brilliant husband. She's a sucker for dark eyes, dark coffee, and dark chocolate.

For a complete reading list, visit
www.piperlawsonbooks.com/books

Subscribe to Piper's VIP email list
www.piperlawsonbooks.com/subscribe

amazon.com/author/piperlawson
bookbub.com/authors/piper-lawson
instagram.com/piperlawsonbooks
facebook.com/piperlawsonbooks
goodreads.com/piperlawson

ACKNOWLEDGMENTS

Sawyer and Liv's story has taken me on a ride I never expected.

Their journey has a different vibe from my previous books, but once these characters started talking in my head, I couldn't stop them.

I have loved every second of my time with the characters at Russell U!

This series wouldn't have happened without the support of my awesome readers, including my ARC team who provides endless enthusiasm, cheerleading, and help spreading the word.

Becca, thank you for talking about my characters like they're real.

Erica, thank you for taking a chance on me and believing in this series.

Tal, Suzanne, and Tina, thank you for your honest feedback, for your cheerleading, and for letting these characters into your heart and seeing their story as clearly as I do.

Thank you Regina for the perfect images to capture the emotion behind this story.

Dani and the Wildfire team, thank you for your sage advice.

Annette, thank you for always being there with a coffee and a bunny when I need them. Don't ever leave me.

And to each of you who read this book...thank you from the bottom of my heart. The best part of author life is having YOU in it.

Love,
Piper

www.ingramcontent.com/pod-product-compliance
Lightning Source LLC
Chambersburg PA
CBHW061600190726

48288CB00007B/2111